About the Author

Robert Dole left his native country, the United States, and went into permanent exile in 1968 at the age of twenty-two, after graduating from Harvard. He lived in Europe for nine years and taught English at the Universities of Metz, Bonn and Lodz. Between 1977 and 2013 he was a professor of English at the Université du Québec à Chicoutimi. He speaks seven languages.

This book is dedicated to
Réjean my spouse, my happiness.

Robert Dole

What Rough Beast

A CIP catalogue record for this title is available from the British Library.

ISBN 9781786936448 (Paperback)
ISBN 9781786936455 (E-Book)
www.austinmacauley.com

First Published (2017)
Austin Macauley Publishers Ltd.
25 Canada Square
Canary Wharf
London
E14 5LQ

THE SECOND COMING

Turning and turning in the widening gyre
The falcon cannot hear the falconer;
Things fall apart; the centre cannot hold;
Mere anarchy is loosed upon the world,
The blood-dimmed tide is loosed, and everywhere
The ceremony of innocence is drowned;
The best lack all conviction, while the worst
Are full of passionate intensity.
Surely some revelation is at hand;
Surely the Second Coming is at hand.
The Second Coming! Hardly are those words out
When a vast image out of *Spiritus Mundi*
Troubles my sight: somewhere in sands of the desert
A shape with lion body and the head of a man,
A gaze blank and pitiless as the sun,
Is moving its slow thighs, while all about it
Reel shadows of the indignant desert birds.
The darkness drops again; but now I know
That twenty centuries of stony sleep
Were vexed to nightmare by a rocking cradle,
And what rough beast, its hour come round at last,
Slouches towards Bethlehem to be born?

William Butler Yeats

By the same author:

Le Cauchemar américain, V.L.B. éditeur

Comment réussir sa schizophrénie, V.L.B. éditeur

Mon Allemagne, Leméac éditeur

Chapter 1: Washington

"For unto us a child is born, unto us a son is given."
Isaiah 9:6

Robin is lying in bed with a cold, this Saturday morning in October 1953. He is seven years old and he is dreaming of a handsome young man who will be his special friend, and accompany him wherever he goes and do whatever he asks him to do. He is having a homoerotic fantasy. He tries to remember when he started daydreaming about his beautiful special friend but is unable to decide in which year of his childhood these longings began.

It is a typical Saturday morning for his family in the northeast section of the District of Columbia. His father is vacuuming the house, his mother is doing the grocery shopping and his brother is playing football with the other boys on the street, some of whom are white and some of whom are Afro-Americans. His brother always plays with boys but Robin most often plays with girls. Robin likes to cook, to knit, to plant flowers, and do all kinds of other things that girls do. He has just asked his mother to buy him a small iron and ironing board so that he can help her with the ironing, but Robin's father will not allow it. His father wants him to be a real man. He says that Robin must learn how to box so that he can defend himself, but Robin refuses. He says that Robin should read the sports page in the newspaper, so that he can have something to talk about with other boys, but Robin has no interest in sports. Robin's brother helps their father with his carpentry projects and Robin helps their mother with her cooking. He learns how to bake bread and loves kneading the dough, getting his fingers stuck with the luscious white paste, and then seeing the loaves rise in the oven. Robin is on his way to becoming an ideal housewife. The only problem is that he is a boy.

The next year, the Supreme Court declares that school segregation based on race is unconstitutional. The schools of the District of Columbia are the first ones in the nation that are integrated. Robin is now in third grade. His neighbourhood is becoming increasingly biracial. His third grade teacher is an Afro-American and many of his friends are as well. One day, his parents tell Robin and his brother that they will have to move to Arlington, Virginia, because the schools are better there.

Their father tells them, "We want you boys to have the best education possible. The quality of education in the schools of Washington is deteriorating with the massive arrival of coloured people from the cotton fields of the South. Many of them cannot even read. We have nothing against the coloured, but we want you boys to have the best opportunities in life, and that means having the best education. Where we will be moving to in Arlington has excellent schools. We will be in an all white neighbourhood and there will be no coloured children in your schools.

"I went to Harvard, as did both of your grandfathers and three of your uncles. You therefore have a good chance of being admitted to Harvard, but we must do our part by offering you the best schools in the area.

"We are Northerners living in the South, Bostonians living in Washington. Both your mother's family and my family have lived in Boston since 1630. I would like to tell you something about your ancestors so that you can be proud of them and so that you can see why your mother and I both expect great things from you.

"I will start with your mother's family. Her father, in whose house we are living, was the first cartographer of *The National Geographic Magazine.* His name was Albert Hoit Bumstead. He also took part in Hiram Bingham's expedition to Machu Picchu. He invented the Bumstead Sun Compass, which Admiral Richard Byrd used for flying to the North and South Poles. His father was Horace Bumstead, who spent his entire life in service to coloured people. He was a major in command of coloured troops, mostly fugitive slaves, during the Civil War. At the age of twenty-four, he led his coloured troops in the final battle of the war, at Richmond, Virginia. After the war he went to Atlanta, Georgia, where he was one of the founders and the second president of Atlanta University, which is still the nation's largest coloured university. He was also one of the founders of the National Association for the Advancement of Coloured People.

"Horace's father-in-law was the famous portrait painter Albert Gallatin Hoit. Hoit's portrait of President Harrison is now hanging in the National Portrait Gallery, a few miles from our house.

"Horace's mother was Lucy Douglas Willis Bumstead and she had three famous siblings. Her brother Nathaniel Parker Willis was one of the most successful authors of the first half of the nineteenth century in America. Her sister Sara was also a famous writer, using the pseudonym Fanny Fern. Her brother Richard was a musician who wrote the melody for the Christmas carol *It Came Upon a Midnight Clear."*

"Now I will tell you about my family. The most famous member of our family is my twin brother, Malcolm. He is a chemist who discovered the difference in the atomic weight of oxygen in water and in air, called the Dole Effect. He also participated in the Manhattan Project, which built the atom bomb. Our ancestor Nathan Haskell Dole was the first American to translate Tolstoy. Another famous Dole was Sanford Ballard Dole, the only president of the Republic of Hawaii. It was he who gave Hawaii to the United States. His nephew, James Dole, started the Dole Pineapple Company, which was to become the Dole Fruit Company. Whenever you see Dole products, please remember that the company was started by our family.

"With such accomplished ancestors, there is no reason that you boys cannot also have fabulous careers and do great things. That is why we want you to have the best education possible. That is why we are moving to Arlington."

It goes without saying that there was never any mention of homosexuality in Robin's illustrious family.

Chapter 2: Arlington

"The prophet which prophesieth of peace, when the word of the prophet shall come to pass, then shall the prophet be known, that the Lord hath truly sent him."
Jeremiah 28:9

Robin is delighted to discover that his new neighbours in Arlington are a family with five girls that he can play with. The Montgomerys come from Utah and they are Mormons. The oldest girl, Mary, is the same age as Robin, ten. The younger sisters are named Margaret, Marcia, Marilyn and Marion. Robin spends all his spare time with the Montgomery girls. He has permanent access to their house and often grabs snacks there. He is treated like a member of the family, like a real prince, as though he were the one son the Montgomery parents had been hoping for.

Mrs. Montgomery explains the Mormon religion to Robin. This is all very exotic for him, since he has been raised as a Unitarian. Religion has always been a subject of discussion in Robin's home especially because his father is religion editor of

The Washington Post. His father is a good Unitarian, which means that he believes absolutely nothing that has not been proven to him from his own experience. But he is also a good religion editor, which requires him to show respect for all religions even if he does not agree with their basic tenets.

Robin's father grew up amongst the Unitarian Harvard elite of Boston, whose most famous spokesmen included Ralph Waldo Emerson, Henry David Thoreau and William Ellery Channing. The fundamental difference between Unitarians and orthodox Christians is their rejection of the Trinity, which is never mentioned in the Bible. From that heresy, it spread to include freethinkers of many different backgrounds. Today there are Jewish Unitarians, humanist Unitarians, atheist Unitarians, and even a few who consider themselves to be Christian Unitarians.

Robin's father likes to think of himself as being a Christian Unitarian, as Emerson had. Yet he holds many ideas that most orthodox Christians would reject. He tells Robin, for example, "There is no such thing as sin. People just make mistakes from time to time. Forgiveness is not always a good thing, since it prevents people from learning from their mistakes. Nobody knows any more about God than anybody else." The basic idea of Christian theology is centered on the idea of sin and forgiveness, so it is hard to imagine why Robin's father wants to continue believing that he is a Christian.

It is quite possible that his father has no concept of sin simply because he had remained a virgin until the age of forty, when he married his childhood sweetheart. When Christians talk about sinning, they usually have in mind their sexual escapades before or outside of the realm of conjugal duty, and Robin's father was never faced with the problem of giving an ethical description to such activity in his own life. He came from a Puritan Calvinist background that went back in time to the sixteenth century. He considers it perfectly normal to resist all temptations of the flesh. He never once discusses sexuality with his two sons.

Robin and his brother go to a series of three Unitarian Sunday schools. The first is at the All Souls' Unitarian Church on Sixteenth Street in the centre of Washington. Then they go to the Unitarian Church in College Park, Maryland, when it is first opened, since it is easier to drive to than the first one. When they move to Arlington, they start attending the Arlington Unitarian Church. There they learn the basic ideas of modern Unitarianism, like "We come together in the love of truth and the spirit of Jesus to worship God and serve man." They are also exposed to the concept that Unitarians worship one God at most. Jesus is not more divine than anyone else. There is a bit of God in everybody. Unitarians worship the fatherhood of God, the brotherhood of man, and the neighbourhood of Boston.

The Mormon religion that Mrs. Montgomery presents to Robin is altogether different from

Unitarianism. Robin learns about prophets, messiahs, heaven, hell, the priesthood, fasting, tithing, the virgin birth, sin, the apocalypse, the resurrection of the dead. But he also learns about Joseph Smith and the Book of Mormon, the lost tribes of Israel coming to America, Brigham Young and Mormon temples. The Mormon Church is really called the Church of Jesus Christ of Latter-day Saints. They are called Latter-day saints because Christ will return to the earth very soon. These are the last days of the old world of sin and misery, which will soon be replaced by heaven on earth when Jesus falls from the sky without a parachute. But when Christ comes in His glory, only those who have been baptised in the Mormon Church will be able to enter the highest heaven.

Between the ages of ten and thirteen, Robin listens reverently to Mrs. Montgomery's proselytizing. He has a real crisis of conscience. How can he remain a good Unitarian and at the same time accept Mrs. Montgomery's ideas? He gives up and announces to his parents, "I want to become a Mormon and be baptised in the Mormon Church so that I can go to the highest heaven when Christ returns. It's going to happen soon and I want to be ready."

The next day, his parents walk over to speak to Mr. and Mrs. Montgomery. They tell their neighbours, "Robin is too young to understand Mormon theology. When he is eighteen years old, he will be old enough. Then he will go and spend a summer with you in Utah and he will decide for himself whether he wants to become a Mormon. He is still too young."

Mrs. Montgomery tells Robin, "I have agreed not to talk to you any more about religion, since your parents say that you are too young."

She has often told Robin, "It is written in the Bible!" She seems to think that the Bible is the supreme authority on everything. So Robin, no longer able to discuss theology with his beloved mentor, decides to read the entire Bible on his own. He does it in secret. Every Saturday morning, when most American children are watching cartoons on television, Robin goes to his bedroom, closes the door and studies the Bible. It takes him two years of Saturday mornings to complete the task.

He reads the Bible to discover the secrets of life as revealed by God to man. He wants most of all to be pleasing to God. At the same time, he discovers stories about the Holocaust that are appearing for the first time in *The Washington Post.* He sees pictures of the cadavers at Auschwitz and asks his mother why these people were killed. She answers, "Because they were Jews." But that does not seem to be an intelligent answer. Jesus, he knows, was also a Jew. In any event, he decides that the entire Bible is one long prayer for peace, and he vows to God that he will be a pacifist his whole life long, that he will never approve of any act of violence or warfare. He would rather go to prison than join any army.

Robin thinks that Jesus's most sublime command is: "Love your enemies" (Matthew 5:44). The Communists are America's enemies, so Robin vows to love the Communists, just because Jesus has told him to do so. He makes this resolution in the shadow of the Pentagon and wonders where it will lead him.

Much of the Bible seems to him to be gibberish. On the other hand, there are certain verses that truly inspire him, that speak directly to his soul, that enlighten him and transform him. He is proud of having read the entire Bible. He thinks that it has given him a solid foundation for his spiritual and intellectual life.

When he finishes reading the Bible at age fourteen, he is distraught by a reality that he can no longer deny. He knows that he is a homosexual. He tells himself, "I am a homosexual. This is my identity. This is what I am." Being a homosexual is considered to be the worst thing possible in the Puritan America of the 1950s. He knows very well that he has always been sexually attracted to boys and men, ever since his early childhood fantasies about his special friend. His desires become more and more explicit. His brain is constantly producing private gay pornographic films. Whenever he sees a beautiful boy, his mind's eye undresses him and beholds him in all his rigid beauty.

Robin has read the Bible in order to be pleasing to God, and now he tells himself that it is impossible to please God since he is a homosexual.

It seems immensely unfair. He tries to clear his mind of all religious ideas by reading atheist authors like Bertrand Russell, Albert Camus and Jean-Paul Sartre. He is now able to read French with ease.

Robin is a real nerd. He gets straight A's in junior high school and senior high school. A friend of his parents knows that Robin is a real whizz kid and suggests that he might have more of an intellectual challenge if he studied at the Phillips Exeter Academy, the most prestigious preparatory school for boys in America. It is located in southern New Hampshire and has the vocation of preparing boys of rich families for studying at Harvard. Robin applies to Exeter, is accepted and asks for a scholarship, which is refused. An aunt comes to the rescue and agrees to pay for Robin's tuition at Exeter.

Chapter 3: Exeter

"What is man, that thou art mindful of him, and the son of man, that thou visitest him?"
Psalm 8:4

The Phillips Exeter Academy is the most prestigious preparatory school in America. Amongst its most famous alumni are Mark Zuckerberg, Dan Brown, John Irving, Jonathan Galassi and David Finkelhor.

When Robin's parents leave him at Exeter in September 1962, at the age of sixteen, the first thing that he does is to walk around the majestic campus and admire the beauty of his new school. He discovers that right across the street from his dormitory, is the Exeter Unitarian Church. He enters it, talks to the minister and says that he would like to sing in the choir. He wants to be a perfect student, make the best grades and be active in many extracurricular activities, like the church choir. He is looking forward to his new courses, especially the French class. This will be his fourth year of studying French.

He shares his room with Matthew, who has spent his whole life in Peru. He comes from an illustrious American family and is perfectly bilingual in English and Spanish. Robin admires people who can speak two or more languages and wants to become a polyglot himself. Thus Matthew immediately becomes something of a hero for him.

One evening in September, Matthew shares his big secret with Robin. "Four of my friends and I decided to have our first sexual experience so we all went to a brothel in Lima. I went to a woman's room, we took off our clothes and all I could do was to do push-ups on the poor woman." Matthew laughs nervously when he tells this story, but Robin senses that Matthew is seriously upset by this experience of sexual impotence. What was meant to be a moment of intense physical pleasure had turned into an experience of extreme psychological pain.

Robin tells himself that this is the opportunity that he has been waiting for, for years. He can finally confide in a sophisticated, cosmopolitan young man who has actually been to a brothel in Lima. He says, "I have a horrible secret that I would like to tell you. You are the only person in the world who will know it. I am a homosexual."

Matthew looks at Robin with amazement. He admires Robin for being so honest and courageous in making this confession. The year is 1962 and these two sixteen year old boys live in a very homophobic boarding school. Matthew has spent his childhood in the macho culture of South America and comes from an old New England Puritan family, as Robin does as well. Robin has admitted to belonging to a detested minority, but Matthew is not outraged. He does not seem to object to living in the same room with a homosexual. Matthew really does not know what to say since this situation is so totally unexpected. Instead of being horrified by sharing a room with a homosexual, he seems intrigued to live with someone who can be so open about his homosexuality. It will be an interesting challenge for Matthew to deal with.

The next evening, Robin is sitting in an armchair reading his textbook for his American history class. He raises his eyes to see Matthew undress in front of him. He is certain that Matthew is shedding his clothes in order to put on his pyjamas and go to bed. But no, Matthew is now walking towards Robin totally naked and with an erection. No force in the universe would be capable of preventing these two boys from coupling. Robin discovers a new use for his mouth; before it was just used for eating, drinking and talking and now this. Overwhelmed by the intense physical pleasure and the excitement of doing something totally forbidden, Matthew erupts immediately.

The boys do not know what to say to each other afterwards. Robin delights in the fantasy of spending years making love with Matthew, whereas Matthew is struggling, trying to come to terms with the idea that he has enjoyed a sexual experience with a boy while he had had no pleasure at all with his Peruvian lady. Matthew's id and super ego are just no longer able to coexist peacefully.

Around ten o'clock the next morning, Robin's housemaster comes to see him and tells him with a wry smile, "You have to go see the Dean." It turns out that Matthew has just gone to the school's infirmary to seek the advice of the school's doctor because he cannot deal with what has happened to him. He cannot admit to himself that he is a homosexual and he certainly cannot live any longer in the same room with a boy who says that he is one.

Robin is distraught at the idea that his big secret is no longer a secret at all. How many people will Matthew tell? How many students and teachers will know that he is a homosexual? What will they be saying about him behind his back?

He goes to the Dean's office. The Dean's secretary leads him in and closes the door. Without any preamble to soften the blow, the Dean says, "Normally you would be thrown out immediately, but because you are a new boy, you will be allowed to continue at Exeter on the condition that you see a psychiatrist every week that you are here. Go to the infirmary and make an appointment."

Before going to the infirmary, Robin walks to the woods near the school to have a good cry without being seen by anyone. His sexual orientation is no longer a secret. In addition to being a sin and a crime, it is now a mental illness. Then he begins to think that it might actually be wonderful that the modern science of psychiatry has developed a way of curing him of his homosexuality and making him a heterosexual. He likes the idea that psychiatrists have achieved such a brilliant type of therapy that can actually make him desire girls instead of boys, while living in an all boys' school without any girls in sight.

Robin is sent to live in a small room at the other end of the campus. To decorate his room, he buys a *Playboy* calendar and sticks the pictures of the naked women on his wall. His goal is not to try to convince the other boys that he is normal, but rather to test the efficacy of psychiatry. If his new psychiatrist is competent, then he will start desiring the *Playboy* bunnies and stop fantasizing about the boys surrounding him.

He has his first appointment with his psychiatrist, Dr. Duncan C. Stephens. He is a man in his sixties, wears a tweed jacket, has a moustache and a big belly, and smokes a pipe. He used to be a physician in the United States Navy. Why he should give up examining young sailors' bodies and spend his retirement in an all boys' school trying to cure young homosexuals, can only remain a matter of conjecture.

During the first meeting, Dr. Stephens asks Robin to tell him about his family. He takes notes. The next week he announces the etiology of Robin's illness. "You are a homosexual because you identified with the women in your family, your mother, your aunt and your grandmother and, because you never had any real contact with your father, who remained aloof and distant. You disappointed him when you were born because he wanted you to be a girl so that he could name you after his own mother. And because your brother was the only one in your family who really loved you and you are seeking a replacement for him."

Robin is shocked to hear that most of his family members did not love him. During the next two years, Robin hears Dr. Stephens make the following psychotherapeutic interventions: "You must marry a woman just like any other man, but you must never tell your wife that you are a homosexual because if you do, she will worry whenever you go bowling with the men in the office." Robin has never wanted to bowl, nor does he want to work in an office. The idea of spending his whole life with a person from whom he has to hide his sexual orientation seems repulsive to him.

"It is not too late for you to change. You can identify with me, who am a real man, and you can see the world through my eyes." Robin detests Dr. Stephens and has no desire whatsoever to identify with him.

"If people know that you are a homosexual, you will never have any friends and you will never have any job." But Robin has already read homosexual authors like André Gide, Oscar Wilde, and James Baldwin, and he would love to have a job like theirs and be surrounded by friends like theirs.

The best part of Robin's life at Exeter is his friendship with David Finkelhor. The two get to know each other at a meeting of the Exeter Peace

Group. They are both pacifists. But more importantly, they have something in common: they both belong to persecuted minorities. David is very conscious of being Jewish. Indeed, his father has told him that he should never ride in a Volkswagen because of the Holocaust. Robin confides his entire story in David. Every week, he tells David about Dr. Stephens's latest pronouncement. "Today he told me that all homosexuals end up bums in the Bowery. Do you have any idea where the Bowery is? How big must it be to contain all the world's homosexuals?"

Needless to say, Robin's desires for the boys around him do not diminish in the least. He quickly realizes that it is useless for any psychiatrist to try to change his sexual orientation and takes the *Playboy* bunnies off his walls, tears them up, and puts them in the trash. The more Dr. Stephens tells him he has to stop being a homosexual, the more he is intent on continuing to be himself. The only effect that the psychotherapy has on him is to make him hate himself more and more. He becomes more and more depressed. Other than David Finkelhor, his only solace is listening to Joan Baez's records.

One day he has a bad cold and has to go to the infirmary. He meets Dr. Heyl, who has been given the task of curing Matthew of his homosexuality. Dr. Heyl does not seem at all interested in treating Robin's cold, but is rather intent on sharing his attitude about homosexuality with him. "All men have certain feminine attributes. For example, I like to make floral arrangements. But that does not mean that I am a homosexual." His concept of homosexuality is obvious: it is impossible for any nice boy coming from a nice family and studying at a nice school, to be a homosexual. Robin would like to ask Dr. Heyl if he has ever had thoughts of performing fellatio on Matthew, his patient, but does not dare.

Robin's depression gets worse and worse. During the summer vacation of 1963, Robin thinks that the only solution to his misery is to pray. He says "God" and God appears. He has a beatific vision. His soul leaves his body, he is in total ecstasy; he sees the Kingdom of God, with God veiled in unapproachable light behind a cloud of angels. This is eternity. He tells himself: this is the God of Abraham, Isaac and Jacob. God tells him: you are my servant. Robin says: I am undone, my life is no longer my own, I am condemned to worship a hallucination for the rest of my life. Robin now knows that Dr. Stephens has made him a schizophrenic instead of turning him into a heterosexual. He realizes that only schizophrenics see what he has seen. He tells himself that this vision will always remain for him the absolute Truth, even if everyone else on earth considers it to be nothing other than a schizophrenic hallucination.

Robin is only seventeen years old and he tells himself that there exists the very real possibility that he will spend his entire life locked up in mental hospitals, thanks to Dr. Stephens. He reads books about mysticism and schizophrenia and tries to understand the relationship between the two.

Robin returns to Exeter in September. He has signed up to take a course in ancient Greek, but after one week God tells him: "You should study religion instead to find out what I want from you." He drops his Greek course and signs up for a religion course. It is in this course that he discovers the books of Paul Tillich, considered by many Christians to be "the greatest theologian since Augustine".[1] The more Robin reads Tillich, the more he is convinced that Tillich has had an experience similar to his own beatific vision, which is now called a schizophrenic hallucination. He considers Tillich to be his mentor. He thinks that Tillich is the only person on earth capable of understanding him correctly, just as he is convinced that he is the only person who has comprehended the real meaning of Tillich's theology.

In May, Robin is accepted at Harvard and his parents jubilate. He is admitted to the Cum Laude Society at Exeter thanks to his excellent grades. He receives the prize for the best student in religion.

During the summer, he keeps his promise to the Montgomery family and hitchhikes to Salt Lake City to spend the summer there and to give the Mormon religion one last chance. He works twelve hours a day painting motel rooms for Mrs. Montgomery's sister with a salary of ninety cents an hour. The Montgomerys insist that he go to church every Sunday, and he chooses to go to the Unitarian

---

[1] Grace Calí. *Paul Tillich First-Hand. A Memoir of the Harvard Years.* Chicago, Exploration Press, 1995, p. 5.

church, where he feels totally at home. At the end of the summer, Mr. Montgomery and another Mormon elder have one last proselytizing session with Robin and it is then that Robin announces that he has chosen not to become a Mormon.

His parents phone up to tell him that he has passed three advanced placement examinations, in French, English and American history and can thus start Harvard as an advanced-placement sophomore. He is delighted. A new life is beginning.

Chapter 4: Harvard

"Take ye heed, watch and pray: for ye know not when the time is. For the Son of man is as a man taking a far journey."
Mark 13:33-34

Robin is so happy to be a new student at Harvard, the University of his family for generations. But his happiness is short lived. On the first day, he goes to the President's reception for new students. He shakes hands with the Dean, who says, "Please come and see me tomorrow morning in my office."

"Don't tell me that I've already done something wrong. I've only been here one day."

"Oh, it's nothing serious. It's just that the FBI wants to talk with you."

Robin immediately guesses the reason for the FBI's investigation. In the previous spring, David Finkelhor and he invited two members of the American Communist Party to give a speech at Exeter. The two Communists had been invited by students at the University of New Hampshire, in Durham, ten miles from Exeter, to give a talk there but the state governor, under pressure from *The*

Manchester Union Leader newspaper, made the students cancel the invitation. David and Robin considered this to be an infringement on the constitutionally guaranteed right of free speech, so they invited the Communists to Exeter and chartered private busses to bring students down from the University of New Hampshire.

Robin's friends prepare for the visit by the FBI by installing hidden tape recorders in his room so that they can capture the agents' words for immortality. When the two men arrive at his door, they immediately invite Robin to come to their car for the interview. One of them says, "We know that you invited two Communists to give a talk at your school and that they advocated the violent overthrow of the United States government. We want you to testify against them."

Robin answers, "But they did not at all advocate the violent overthrow of anything. They simply talked about the history of the labour movement in the United States. Sorry I can't help you." Now Robin knows that he will always be observed by the FBI, as well as by the Communists.

Robin enjoys his study of English Literature, Philosophy and German. His first semester as an advanced-placement sophomore passes well enough, despite his morbid sexual frustration, for which he has no solution. There is no gay scene anywhere that he knows of. He is afraid that if he attempts to seduce any Harvard student, he will be expelled. He continues to hear the words of his first psychiatrist: “If people know that you are a homosexual, you will never have any friends and you will never have any job.”

During the first week of March, he sees an announcement saying that Paul Tillich will be coming back to Harvard to give a sermon on March 28th. God immediately tells him: “Thou hast to tell Tillich about thy vision of two years ago. That is why I revealed myself to thee, while remaining veiled. He is a true prophet, and he will know what thy vision meant and what thou must do. This is an order.”

On March 27th, Robin closes himself in his room and writes a 27 page essay for Tillich entitled *The Phenomenological Proof of God*. He refers to Tillich’s books, the Bible, mystics, poets, philosophers and theologians and quotes them in English, French and German.

The next morning at seven o’clock he goes to look for the 78 year old world renowned theologian. He knows he has to be somewhere on the campus, but where? He goes to the Harvard Divinity School where he finds a student. “Do you know where Tillich is?”

The student must be surprised by such a strange question at such an unlikely hour, but Robin is even more surprised that the student has the answer: “In the Hotel Continental.”

Robin runs to the Hotel Continental. The Holy Ghost is in his soul and has turned his feet into wings. Robin knows that the three of them, God, Tillich and himself, are coming together to usher in God's Kingdom on earth. No force in the universe can prevent God, Tillich and Robin from getting together and making a holy covenant that will change humanity forever.

Robin goes to the reception desk at the hotel and asks, "Can you give me Tillich's room number?" He is surprised that the attendant gives him what he wants, since it takes about as much audacity for a Protestant to ask for Tillich's whereabouts as it would take a Catholic to ask in which room the Pope is sleeping.

Robin goes upstairs and knocks on the door. Tillich's wife, Hannah, opens the door and makes no effort to hide her anger and sense of insecurity by being awakened by a perfect stranger. She asks bluntly, "Wer are you? Wer are you?"

Robin knows enough German to realize that she is asking him *who* he is and not *where* he is. The only problem is that ever since the Holy Ghost has invaded his soul, he no longer knows who he is. All that he can answer is, "I have written an essay for Dr. Tillich."

"One moment," she says and closes the door.

Robin sits in the corridor waiting. He is doing God's will. He is delighted but also full of trepidation. His entire future depends on Tillich's reaction to his essay.

Finally, the theologian opens his door, which is next to Hannah's, and Robin hands him his essay in a brown envelope. "Please read this," he says.

Tillich tells him, "Go to the reception and wait for me there."

Robin does as he has been told. While sitting there, he tells himself that he is making a covenant with Tillich that will become the purpose of his life. He is making a commitment from which there will never be any form of release. He is doing God's bidding, after all.

He thinks about Tillich's theology. Ever since 1920, Tillich has been saying that his theology is one of the *kairos*. This Greek word means "the propitious moment." But in the Greek New Testament it specifically means the propitious moment for the advent of the Son of Man, as seen in Mark 13:33. The Son of Man is also called the Second Coming of Christ, the Messiah, the Lord's Anointed and the Prince of Peace.

Robin thinks that Tillich must believe what the Mormons had told him in his childhood: the return of Christ is imminent. These are the latter days. When he puts all these ideas together, he realizes that he might actually be in the most unusual position of applying for the job of Messiah. This thought makes him horrified for he knows that it means that he is going insane. He is afraid of being locked up in insane asylums for the rest of his life.

After about a half an hour, Tillich comes down and sits next to him. Without looking at Robin, Tillich says roughly, "You have no right to write about zese matters. Zere are people who have spent zeir whole lives studying zese matters. You have no right." Robin thinks that Tillich is not being serious or sincere. He knows that Tillich is famous for his sentence: "Accept that you are accepted." He believes that Tillich could never tell him that he has to accept being rejected.

Then Tillich turns his head, looks Robin right in the eye, and gives him an ecstatic smile that says more than all the words in the world could say. It is a smile that will accompany Robin throughout his life. Robin knows that Tillich has confidence in him and that this confidence reflects his faith in God.

Tillich then tells him, "Send it to me when you have finished it."

"Yes?" Robin asks.

"Yes," Tillich answers.

Yes, yes, yes, yes, yes.

As Robin leaves Tillich, he looks at his feet and wonders where they will take him, today, tomorrow, and the rest of his life. Wherever they go, they will be feet sent on their way by Tillich's smile.

Robin becomes "the great unknown One"[2] , for whom Tillich has been waiting all his life. He is

---

[2] Hannah Tillich. *From Time to Time.* New York: Stein and Day, 1974, p 104.

also Tillich's angel of death, since he will die just seven months later.

Four hours later Tillich gives the last sermon of his life, entitled "The Right to Hope." He concludes with these words: "The Son of Man is in our presence. He will come as a beggar. The fate of the world depends on how He matures."

Robin knows that Tillich is talking about him.

He goes back to his room in Adams House and writes another sixty pages of his essay with his typewriter. What he had written before meeting Tillich was lucid, coherent and cohesive. What he writes after meeting him is unmitigated delirium. Robin has fallen into the hell of an acute paranoid schizophrenic psychosis. In his dementia, he raves on and on about what he will do to save the world when he is sitting on his throne of glory and is recognized by all the peoples of the earth as being the long awaited Saviour. He takes his 96 page essay to the Post Office and sends it to Tillich.

Robin comes back to his room. He shares a suite of three bedrooms with David Finkelhor and another student. He is frightened out of his mind. He tells David that he has to sleep in the same bed with him. He is afraid to sleep alone. The world is coming to an end and it is all his fault. David goes to spend the night in the room of another friend and the next day goes to the Stillman Infirmary to inform a doctor that his roommate has become psychotic.

Three men come to collect Robin. Two are Harvard administrators and the third is an old Harvard policeman who looks Irish. Robin cannot understand why these men want to lock up the Messiah in an insane asylum. Have they not read Tillich's books about the *kairos* and the visible sign of grace that the world needs? They seem to be totally ignorant of Tillich's "shaking of the foundations" and his "final catastrophe of world history." He refuses to go. The three men tell him that he has no choice. Robin says, "I will let you take me away on the condition that you say the Lord's Prayer with me." The old Irish policeman kneels and he and Robin say the prayer together while the two intellectuals look on with cynicism.

Robin is driven away and locked up for fifteen months, a victim of America's homophobic psychiatrists.

Chapter 5: McLean

"The prophet is a fool, the spiritual man is mad."
Hosea 9:7

McLean Hospital is the most prestigious mental hospital in America. Among its most famous patients have been Robert Lowell, Sylvia Plath, James Taylor, Ray Charles and John Nash. Thus, within the period of one year, Robin has lived in America's most prestigious preparatory school, America's most prestigious University and America's most prestigious mental hospital. Despite all its prestige, McLean is a medieval insane asylum, no better than Bedlam.

When he enters his ward, North Belknap 2, he runs around like a mouse in a cage. There is one face that he recognizes, Matthew's. If only Exeter's homophobic psychiatrists could see the results of their medicine. Their two patients, whom they tried to cure of the memory of having loved each other, are now locked up on the same day, in the same ward, of the same mental hospital.

Robin's fall into the horrors of an acute paranoid schizophrenic psychosis is merciless. He has a hallucination of hell, which is dark, chaotic, and more frightful than can be imagined. He runs around naked, shouts eschatological prophecies and scatological curses, beats his head, hands and feet against the floor leaving stigmata on his hands and feet. Finally, three men come into his room. Two hold him down while the third one shoots his buttocks with a massive dose of tranquilizers.

When he wakes up he does not know how many hours or days he has been sleeping in his chemically produced slumber. His parents are in his room. His mother is crying. She blames herself for having driven her son insane. She does not know that she never did anything wrong, that it is Dr. Stephens who is to blame. Robin cannot tell her since he is unable to talk coherently.

He is given specials for one month. Specials are young female nurses who sit with him in his room, twenty-four hours a day. There are three of them per day, each working a shift of eight hours.

After one month, he is allowed to share a normal room with a roommate who smokes constantly and never says anything. It is then that he has his first lucid thought. He tells himself: My first psychiatrist has driven me insane. The only way for me to find sanity is to live as a real homosexual and do everything that Dr. Stephens told me that I should not do.

Robin makes certain basic rules for himself. He vows that he will never discuss homosexuality with any psychiatrist since he knows that they all think that homosexuality is a mental illness and he disagrees with them. He promises himself also that he will never tell a psychiatrist that a German theologian named Paul Tillich thinks that he is the Son of Man because if he does, he will never be released. The two major issues on his mind remain his deep dark secrets.

Robin decides that he will keep his faith in God, and to help him do so all that he has to do, is to keep his spiritual eye fixed on Tillich's beatific smile. On October 23, 1965, he reads in *The New York Times* that Tillich died the day before, at the age of 79. He tells himself that this is not true; it was just his body that died. Tillich and Robin made a transmigration of souls on March 28, 1965, Tillich being 78 years old and Robin being 18. Tillich's soul left his body and entered Robin's body. The Germans call this form of metempsychosis *Seelenwanderung,* the wandering of a soul from one person to another.

But Robin does not want to be Tillich's Messiah. First of all, he is still a Unitarian and Unitarians do not believe in messiahs. Secondly, he does not want to be crucified.

So he prays to God to find out how he can keep his promise to Tillich to bring about Tillich's socialist apocalypse, for Tillich is a Marxist. God tells Robin: "Tillich, Yeats and the Mormons are right in saying that the twentieth century is the *kairos*, the appropriate moment in history for the return of Christ. But thou art not Christ. Thy task is to go and find the real Christ. I will give thee a clue.

He will be the most beautiful young man that thou hast ever seen. I will also give thee a promise. He will be the special friend that thou dreamed about when thou wert seven years old. Thou shouldest love him, honour him, serve him, worship him, and he will save thee. He will be thy road to mental health. Be patient, and when thou leavest this mental hospital, thou wilt discover him. I promise thee."

Every week, David Finkelhor comes to visit Robin. He brings him news of the outside world and books, but most importantly he brings him hope and love. He saves Robin's life. Psychiatrists have never understood that any mental illness is also a spiritual illness. The only cure for a spiritual illness is faith, hope and love, as the Apostle Paul says. Tillich's blessing gave Robin faith in God, and David Finkelhor provided the hope and love. All psychotherapy and psychiatric medicines were useless.

One day Robin makes a request to David. "Please bring me Marcel Proust in French. What could be better than reading *À la recherche du temps perdu* while I am locked up here wasting my time?"

The psychiatrists do everything they can to convince Robin that his life is over, that he should expect to spend the rest of his days in their institutions, taking their psychiatric medicine and following their psychotherapy. There are many patients at McLean who have been here for ten years, twenty years, thirty years, even forty years. Robin knows one lady who was locked up by her husband, a psychiatrist working at McLean, forty years ago, so that he could live in peace with his mistress.

One psychiatrist tells Robin, "We have never seen any patient so severely mentally ill as you were when you arrived here."

Another one says, "You must never go back to Harvard."

Robin is filled with tranquilizers, Stelazine and Thorazine, which turn him into a fat, constipated zombie.

After two months of waiting, he is given his first psychiatrist. She is called Dr. Maria Lorenz. She is a little old lady with curly black hair who sits behind a big desk in the Administration Building. She smokes Parliament cigarettes constantly and does not say anything. She reminds Robin of the old catatonic patients that he sees everywhere he looks. After six weeks of getting nowhere with her, he demands to have another psychiatrist.

The next one, much to his surprise and relief, seems to be capable of speech. And he is sympathetic. He takes so many notes about what Robin says and also smokes constantly, but Robin likes him. His name is Dr. Trivus and he is young and looks like a mouse with his funny glasses and belly.

Robin makes a friend. One day, sitting in the coffee shop reading Proust, he sees a girl about five years older than himself, with long brown hair, a pretty face and good figure, come up to him. "I saw you reading in French, and I thought that we might have something in common," she tells him. "I also read French, as well as Italian."

"Wow, you actually know Italian!" says Robin. "I would love for you to teach me Italian."

Her name is Maria Maddalena Pavvi and she comes from a family of Italian immigrants who became rich in the construction business. She is a student at Boston University majoring in French and Italian.

After a few Italian lessons, Maria Maddalena tells Robin her story. "Five years ago I attempted to hang myself after an unhappy relationship with a woman. My parents brought me to McLean and I have been here ever since. My psychiatrist's name is Dr. Weintraub. When I first met him, he put his little finger in my little finger and told me that we would work out this together. Then he gave me electric shock therapy."

Robin confides his story to Maria Maddalena, which is easy to do because they have so much in common. They are both homosexuals and they are both nerds who love books and languages. They form a friendship that will last forever. He even shares with her his story about Tillich. He says, "Tillich thought that I am the Son of Man, but God has recently told me that the true Christ is someone else and he has given me the task of finding him. Perhaps you can help me."

After thirteen months of this torture, Robin's parents' insurance policy runs out of money, and he has to be transferred to a less expensive mental hospital. They choose one in Baltimore, which is near their home in Arlington, because they know a doctor there. Robin is immediately asked if he wants to continue taking tranquilizers and he answers with an emphatic 'No'. After two months, he is released and immediately returns to Cambridge.

Chapter 6: Cambridge

"Now there was leaning on Jesus' bosom one of his disciples, whom Jesus loved."
(John 13:23)

When Robin returns to Cambridge, he immediately gets in touch with Maria Maddalena, who has just been released from McLean. They decide to take a course together at the Harvard summer school called Absurdity in French Literature.

One day during the first week, Robin walks out into Harvard Square. It is a hot, sunny June day. He spots the most handsome man that he has ever seen. He is so beautiful that he outshines the dawn. The heavens open up and an angel descends from heaven and flies around the young man's head. It is undoubtedly the Angel Moroni! He tells Robin: "I have a message for thee from God on high. He says, 'This is my truly beloved Son, in whom I am well pleased. Thou shouldest love Him, honour Him, and worship Him, and He will be thy Saviour'."

The next day, he goes back to Harvard Square and the Lord's Anointed is there again. He has a job as a sandwich man, carrying a notice advertising books on sale at the Paperback Booksmith on Brattle Street. He tells Maria Maddalena that he has discovered the true Christ, the special friend that God had promised him when he was locked up at McLean Hospital. Maria Maddalena insists on meeting him.

The next day the two of them go to Harvard Square together and Robin tells Maria Maddalena, "I want to see if you can spot him." Within seconds the Angel Moroni makes a second apparition and points to Robin's Saviour across the street. Maria Maddalena exclaims, "There he is!"

"You are absolutely right. God has given you the same inspiration that he gave me." The young man has wide shoulders, an athletic body, a rugged face, sideburns, and bushy brown hair. He is the quintessence of masculine beauty.

Maria Maddalena says, "We must not let this moment go by. Come, let's go talk to your Saviour. This is the road to mental health."

The two cross the street and approach their Adonis, holding hands. Maria Maddalena does all the talking. She and Robin's messiah talk on and on about trivial things and then all of a sudden, she says, "Young man, my friend here would like to tell you that he finds you an aesthetically pleasing ornament to Harvard Square." Robin has never been so embarrassed in his life. He wishes that the earth would open up and swallow him whole. But this is Maria Maddalena's concept of the road to mental health. Before he knows it, she is giving Robin's address to the stranger and inviting him to come to Robin's place that evening. This is how Robin meets Mark Frechette.

Much to Robin's surprise, Mark actually comes to his apartment on Fairmont Avenue that evening. Robin gets straight to the point, and tells Mark his story. "Four years ago my roommate in prep school seduced me and then the school made me see a psychiatrist for two years to cure me of my homosexuality. But instead of turning me into a heterosexual, the shrink transformed me into a schizophrenic, and I had to spend fifteen months in mental hospitals. I just got out last week. The only way for me to achieve any kind of mental health is by making love with you."

Mark has a similar story: "A Roman Catholic priest named Father Laurence Francis Xavier Brett started sexually abusing me when I was fourteen and living in Fairfield, Connecticut. I dropped out of school and ran away to Greenwich Village. I came home last Christmas and my parents had me locked up in a mental hospital called the Hartford Institute of Living. They sent three thugs to my bedroom and they forced me into their van. I managed to escape last week by making love with a black nurse in an elevator on the condition that she gave me her keys to the hospital. I was a straight-A student until that priest came into my life. My parents once tried to sue the Vatican for their priest having ruined my life, but of course they got nowhere with it. I need a place to stay."

Robin needs Mark's love and Mark needs a place to stay. For the next two years they live together and hang out together first at Robin's apartment on Fairmont Avenue, then at his room in Adams House on the Harvard campus during the fall session of 1966, and then in the years 1967 and 1968 in Robin's apartment on Putnam Avenue. Mark does odd jobs, Robin studies and does the cooking. They smoke marijuana together and they make love together. Robin is twenty years old now, and Mark, eighteen.

Robin is absolutely certain that he is making love with the Son of God. He thinks of the ecstasy that he had known in 1963 when he saw the Kingdom of God and he compares it to the ecstasy he knows holding Mark's body next to his own. The first ecstasy was entirely spiritual, but what he knows with Mark is both spiritual and physical. He had never known that pleasure could be so intense. He can actually feel Mark driving away his demons of schizophrenia and paranoia. His Saviour lies on top of him and Robin thanks God for sending him His Son. He never doubts that Mark is the Second Coming of Christ, the rough beast whose advent Yeats prophesizes.

Mark and Robin share a profound prophetic anger with the adult world and especially with the United States. It is God's wrath. They both know that their lives have been broken by men in authority, one a priest and the other, a psychiatrist. They detest the American way of life, its materialism, its hypocrisy, its superficiality, its conformism, its competitiveness, its violence, its rules and regulations, its racism, its militarism, its war in Vietnam, everything. They are hippies in their philosophy, in their way of life and in their dreams.

And they love each other. One day, out of the blue, Mark tells Robin, "I have an undying love and admiration for you." These words remain locked in Robin's heartstrings and they accompany him wherever he goes.

Robin's mother talks to Mark on the telephone and later tells him, "I am certain that Mark is doing you a world of good." Mothers know everything. She is the only adult who actually encouraged Robin to live as a homosexual. She also tells him, "You will never be able to buy health insurance in the United States."

Another time, Robin speaks with Mark's father on the telephone. He has nothing good to say about his son. With a father like that, he tells himself, no wonder Mark has psychological troubles.

Robin decides to start Harvard's first homosexual discussion group. He goes to the office of *The Harvard Crimson* and hands the announcement of the first meeting to the receptionist. She reads it and looks horrified. She declares, "I really don't know if we can publish this. I will have to ask the editor." She disappears and then returns with the surprising news that it can be published. Of Harvard's 21,000 students, only two come to the meeting, Robin and another undergraduate.

In May 1968 Robin tells Mark, "I am leaving the United States forever next month, as soon as I get my Harvard diploma. I shall go to Europe, starting in Ireland. With my Harvard diploma and my knowledge of French, German and Italian, I should not have any trouble getting jobs teaching English as a foreign language."

Mark becomes angry with Robin for the first time. He says, "You will spend your life as a tourist, living out of a suitcase. America needs you."

"America needs me, you say. After what America has done to you and to me and to the Vietnamese and to the Blacks, why should either of us have any loyalty to America? Don't you realise that neither you nor I will ever be able to buy health insurance in this fucked-up country just because a priest and a psychiatrist drove us crazy? Do you want to spend the rest of your life as a welfare beggar? America is going down the tubes, and I do not want to go with it. This country has no future. It will get worse and worse, and you know this just as well as I do. But one thing I can tell you is that I will always be grateful to you, that I will always love you. You have brought me happiness and mental health. You have done for me what no psychiatrist could ever do. If I could take you with me, I would.

"Before I leave America, there is one last secret that I want to share with you. Two days before I was locked up at McLean, I gave an essay to a German theologian called Paul Tillich. I am sure that you have never heard of him. After studying his books for six years, I now realise that he was a schizophrenic Marxist. He had to hide both his schizophrenia and his Marxism so that he could have his career in American universities. He taught at the Union Theological Seminary in New York and at Harvard.

"How do I know that he was a schizophrenic? It's because he describes with such perfect accuracy what happens in a mystical schizophrenic hallucination that it is obvious that he has had one himself. At least it is obvious to other schizophrenics. As a schizophrenic, I am able to recognize and understand schizophrenia in other people, whereas normal people are not able to. I have discovered in my readings that Tillich was locked up in a mental hospital during the First World War and I am certain that it was for schizophrenia.

"Tillich was also a patriotic German whose mortal enemies during the First World War were the Americans, the British, the French and the Canadians. I am convinced that during the 32 years that he was living in America, he felt that he had been forced to seek refuge in the land of his enemy.

"As for his Marxism, let me give you some examples. This book here, which I borrowed from the Widener Library, is called *Die sozialistische Entscheidung*. That means *The Socialist Decision.*

This book is pure Marxism. It was because of this book that the Nazis fired Tillich from his job as Professor at the University of Frankfurt. Tillich never allowed this book to be translated into English during his lifetime so that he would not be fired from his teaching positions in America. Thank God that I can read German."

"Let me give you some examples of his Marxist ideas. He says, 'Dictatorship appears to be the radical antithesis of democracy, but it is not. Dictatorship is based on democracy'.[3]

"Can you imagine that Harvard would have let Tillich teach here if they knew that he was in favour of dictatorship?

"Here's another quotation for you, Mark. 'Even world communism is teleologically related to the Spiritual Community'. [4] Here he is praising Communism while profiting to the maximum from American capitalism. What a hypocrite!

"Listen to this. 'The romantic type which identifies religion and socialism seems, finally to have found a soil that has been intellectually and historically prepared for it in Russia'[5]. Now, if he had so much admiration for Russian socialism, why didn't he go and live in Russia or even in East

---

[3] Paul Tillich, *Political Expectation*, Macon, Georgia: Mercer University Press, 1971, p. 110.
[4] Paul Tillich, *Systematic Theology,* Chicago: Chicago University Press, 1963, vol. 3, p. 155.
[5] Paul Tillich, *Political Expectation.* Macon, Georgia: Mercer University Press, 1971, p. 45.

Germany, near where he was born? Bertold Brecht chose to live in socialist East Germany, but it seems that Tillich preferred his American salary.

"But my favourite sentence from Tillich is this one. 'The so-called "iron-curtains" which we build to a certain extent by not admitting books from the East, etc., are attempts to keep the people in one definite tradition and to prevent it from touching other traditions'.[6] We all know, Mark, that "We" did not build the Iron Curtain, that it was the Communists who built it, and their purpose was to keep people in socialist countries from escaping to capitalist ones. Tillich was totally crazy, saying that we in the West built the Berlin Wall so that people here could not read Marx and Engels and Lenin. You can get any book by any socialist author you want in libraries and bookstores in the West.

"The reason that I am telling you this, Mark, is that Tillich said in the Harvard Church the day that he met me, that the Son of Man is in our presence. This means the Messiah. The Messiah is supposed to humble the rich and exalt the poor, which is just what socialism does. Tillich kept saying that 'Jesus was the first socialist'[7]. Well, I think that Jesus was the first pacifist and I have no enthusiasm for Marxist-inspired socialism.

---

[6] Paul Tillich. *A History of Christian Thought.* New York: Simon and Schuster, 1967, p. 140.

[7] Paul Tillich. *Political Expectation.* Macon, Georgia: Mercer University Press, 1971, p. 40.

"So Tillich wanted me to bring about what he calls the Final Catastrophe of World History[8], his Marxist apocalypse that would replace American capitalist imperialism by his German religious socialism, but I want to have no part of it.

"When I was in the loony bin, God told me that I would discover the real Christ and that He would save my life with his love. That means you. If you want to be the Messiah, all you have to do is to make some revolutionary gesture and then proletarian Americans, whom Tillich calls 'the revolutionary masses,' will rise up and overthrow their capitalist oppressors. It's all up to you. I'm leaving."

Mark answers, "You're totally out of your mind, but that is why I love you."

"Let's face it, Mark. Have you ever thought what psychiatrists would do with Jesus if he were alive today? They would do with him exactly what they did with you and me. They would lock him up in an insane asylum and stuff him full of tranquilizers. Perhaps they would even give him electric shock treatments or, better still, a lobotomy. If psychiatrists had existed two thousand years ago, there would never have been any Christian religion."

This is what Mark says about the years that he and Robin spent together in an interview with *The*

---

[8] Paul Tillich. *Theology of Peace.* Louisville, Kentucky: Westminster/John Knox Press, 1990, p. 132.

Boston Globe: "In 1966, 67 and 68 there was something happening. There was incredible interchange. We haven't changed. Everybody else is gone. Where did they go?"[9]

[9] *The Boston Globe*, September 9, 1973.

Chapter 7: Ireland

"Remember this day, in which ye came out of Egypt, out of the house of bondage; for by strength of hand the Lord brought you out of this place."
Exodus 13:3

When he leaves the United States, his house of bondage, Robin goes straight to his grandmother's village in West Cork called Caheragh, between Drimoleague and Skibbereen. His mother's mother, Annie Sweeney, was born there in 1871. Robin remembers her. He and his family actually lived in her house in Washington. Robin was four years old when she died.

She and two of her sisters emigrated to Boston around 1899. Their parents had survived the potato famine. When she married Albert Hoit Bumstead in 1901, the two bought a two-hundred-year-old farmhouse in Townsend Harbour, Massachusetts, about thirty miles northwest of Boston. It was called Townsend Harbour because it had been a harbour on the Underground Railroad. Annie and Albert chose to live so far from Boston to avoid having to tell his stern Calvinist parents that he had married an Irish Catholic. Their first child, Robin's mother, was baptised a Catholic whereas the other four children were baptised in the Congregational Church. Under so much pressure from her new family, Annie converted to Protestantism.

Annie never spoke to her children about her Irish childhood, as though she were ashamed of it. After she died, Robin's uncle went to Caheragh and got to know the people there. Then one of Robin's aunts went there as well and gave a fair amount of money for the construction of the new Catholic Church there.

Right after saying goodbye to Mark, Robin takes the airplane from Boston to London, the train from London to Liverpool, the ferry from Liverpool to Dublin, the train from Dublin to Cork, the bus from Cork to Drimoleague, and then hitchhikes to Caheragh. When he gets off the bus in Drimoleague, the conductor tells him, "Welcome home," and Robin's heart melts with gratitude to God for having brought him safely home after all his trials and troubles in the land of his birth.

The Ireland of the Welcomes. Céad míle fáilte.

He goes to the home of the McNeil family, since his aunt had given him their address. He is received like a long-lost prince, an Odysseus whose voyage has come to its destination. He is overwhelmed by the kindness of the people, their good humour, their sense of enjoying life while only possessing basic material goods. The McNeils live in a small cottage with a turf fire. There is electricity and running water, but no internal water closet. The outhouse, called the jacks, will have to do. There is a radio, but no telephone or television. Everyone seems so happy. They talk constantly, and in the evening there is a ceili. The pub is so full that the men have to stand up. The Guinness is good for Robin. Robin loves the smell of the smoke from the turf fires. He loves the fuchsia blooming everywhere. He loves the hills, he loves the vales, he loves the ocean, he loves the rivers, he loves the fog, he loves the rain. He loves everything in Ireland.

Robin comes to a decision. Never again will he live in the United States. If he had the possibility, he would refrain from living in the twentieth century anywhere on earth. The paradise that he has discovered in West Cork is straight out of the Middle Ages. Robin renounces all the conspicuous consumption and ostentatious affluence of his unhappy fatherland. He promises himself to avoid rich people, sophisticated people, powerful people, fashionable people. All he wants is to live amongst simple, down-to-earth, normal, humble people.

When Robin was at Harvard, he had known classmates with all sorts of ambitions. Some wanted to become rich lawyers or doctors or famous professors. One even told him that he wanted to be the first Jewish governor of Maine. When he was nineteen years old, Robin had only one ambition. He wanted to spend his life outside mental hospitals. He knew that his psychiatrists thought that this would be impossible, and he was determined to prove them wrong. Since he left the

United States in 1968 at the age of twenty-two, he has never consulted a psychiatrist or taken psychiatric medicine. He has an inner resource that no doctor could expect. He has faith in God. He knows that God loves him and that God is on his side. He has God's wind in his sails, and that is the most powerful spiritual medicine possible. All the psychiatric medicine in the world cannot come close to it.

He goes back to Dublin and rents a one-room flat in the attic of a Georgian house on Warrington Place between Upper Mount Street and Lower Mount Street. He has a turf fire, and has to bring up water from the ground floor. For his toilet, he has the jacks in the back garden.

During the mornings, he teaches French at an all-boys' Catholic secondary school in Cabinteely. In the afternoons he studies at Trinity College in the Higher Diploma in Education programme. In the evenings he drinks Guinness at McDaid's. He has the time of his life.

Robin loves the English spoken in Dublin and soon develops an Irish accent. When American tourists meet him, they think that he is Irish.

He gets to know Seanie Lambe, who is a member of the Irish Communist Party. They take part together in demonstrations against the war in Vietnam. One evening, two Vietnamese Communists give a lecture and Robin serves as their interpreter since they speak French but not English.

If only the FBI could see him now! Seanie and he will remain friends forever.

In the following years, Robin takes courses in the Irish language. He becomes a citizen of Ireland in 1974. His mother gets together all the birth certificates necessary to prove that he is the grandson of a person born in Ireland, which is sufficient to obtain Irish citizenship. He will renounce his United States citizenship after the election of George W. Bush in the year 2000.

In 1970 Robin leaves Ireland and moves to the Continent where he will teach English as a foreign language in universities in France, Germany, and Poland. He improves his French, German and Italian, and adds Spanish, Polish and Russian to his repertoire. He manages to do all this because God is good to him.

Chapter 8: Zabriskie Point

"They all say unto him, Let him be crucified."
(Matthew 27:22)

One day in the summer of 1968, while Robin is in Ireland, Mark Frechette is standing at a bus stop on Massachusetts Avenue in Cambridge. He is "swearing at a man who had thrown a geranium at a quarrelling couple."[10] A talent scout working for Michelangelo Antonioni just happens to witness the scene. He invites Mark into his car, tells him that he is not trying to pick him up and explains that he is working for a famous Italian movie director who wants to make a film about American hippies and revolutionaries. The talent scout has been given the job of finding the angriest young man in America.

The talent scout tells an upper scout, "I've got one that really knows how to hate!"[11]

Antonioni comments, "It is not hate. The young men, they say they are through with this country, that they don't believe in it any more, but they do… This is one of Mark's problems in the film. You

[10] *The Boston Globe*, March 10, 1970
[11] *The New York Times,* December 15, 1968

know, in America someone like Nixon is responsible for exactly his opposite: young people so good they don't lie or make stupid promises."[12]

Zabriskie Point is really about Mark. He does not have to act, he just plays himself. He is acclaimed as being America's new James Dean, a rebel, angry against a cruel, meaningless, unjust society. He plays the role of a revolutionary who kills a policeman during a student demonstration against the war in Vietnam in a Californian university. He then steals an airplane, flies over a desert, discovers a girl named Daria Halprin, makes love with her, returns the airplane to the airport from where he had stolen it, and is killed by the police.

Mark does not like the film. He says, "Antonioni didn't represent reality. It is all surface phenomena, a period piece, part of the prehistoric past… The whole movie embarrassed me… I thought the love scene was a total disaster… I didn't like any of it."[13]

Mark becomes internationally famous. The film is shown all over the world, dubbed into Europe's major languages. Robin sees the film for the first time in Florence with Mark speaking Italian, then in Cologne with him speaking German, and then in Paris with Mark speaking French. He will have to wait until he moves to Canada in 1977 to see the original English version.

---

[12] *The New York Times*, December 15, 1968

[13] *The Boston Globe*, March 10, 1970

Then Mark makes another movie, directed by another Italian, Francesco Rosi. In Italian it is called *Uomini contro* and in English, *Many Wars Ago.* It comes out in 1970, right after *Zabriskie Point.*

After a brief moment of glory, Mark is more or less forgotten by the public. He lives in the Mel Lyman community at Fort Hill in Boston.

On August 30, 1973, Mark decides that the moment has come for him to make his revolutionary gesture. He and two of his friends attempt to commit an armed robbery at the New England Merchants National Bank in Roxbury. Mark's rifle is not loaded. His friend Christopher Thien, only fifteen years old, is shot and killed by the police. This visceral protest against American capitalism of course reminds one of Jesus overturning the tables of the money changers in the temple (Matthew 21:12).

When he is arrested, Mark makes this statement: "I am afflicted by a political conscience. We did it as a revolutionary act of political protest. We had been watching the Watergate hearings on television and we saw John Dean tell the truth, and we saw Mitchell and Stans lie about it. We saw the apathy and we felt an intense rage. They did not know the truth and they did not want to know the truth. We know the truth and wanted to show it to them. Because banks are federally insured, robbing that bank was a way of robbing Richard Nixon without hurting anybody. There was no way to stop what was going to happen. We just reached the point where all that the three of us wanted to do was hold up a bank. And besides, standing there with a gun, cleaning out a teller's cage – that's about as fucking honest as you can get, man.

"It would be a direct attack on everything that is choking this country to death."

When he hears the news, Robin is at home with his parents in New Hampshire, on summer vacation from his work as a lecturer in English at the University of Bonn. He wonders if Mark remembers when Robin told him, that Mark was Tillich's Messiah and that he had to set off a Marxist revolution in America in order to replace American capitalist imperialism with German religious socialism. Was Mark actually trying to create Tillich's "final catastrophe of world history" by making a socialist apocalypse?

Robin visits Mark at the Charles Street Jail. When Mark sees that Robin continues to love and worship him as much now as ever before, he tells him, "I really fucked you up."

"You didn't fuck me up, Mark. You saved my life! If it hadn't been for you, I would still be locked up in insane asylums.

"It's more likely that I fucked you up, telling you that you had to make a revolutionary gesture to bring about Tillich's socialist apocalypse. Do you remember when I read to you his line about America's 'revolutionary masses'? Well, I suppose Tillich would have thought that Americans would rise up in arms against their capitalist oppressors when they saw you attempt to rob your local bank. Maybe we were both fucked up by Tillich. How could Americans be so naïve and let an avowed Marxist teach in universities here for thirty-two years?"

"Mark, I want to ask you to forgive me for giving you all that Marxist apocalypse bullshit. I feel that I am to blame for you being here."

Robin starts to cry. Mark says, "Calm down. You'll get over it. I'll be okay."

Mark is sentenced to a term of ranging from six to fifteen years at the Walpole State Prison, but he ends up at the Norfolk prison.

Robin returns to Bonn and corresponds with Mark. He sends him books and magazine subscriptions.

In 1974, Robin comes back to America for his summer vacation. He visits Mark at Norfolk. Mark tells him, "I'm doing okay here, except for two inmates who have been harassing me. They have been making advances, I mean sexual advances. Sometimes one, then other times the other. Once they tried it together. Other than that, I'm managing. I really dig some of the books that you send me."

Robin returns to Germany on a Russian boat called *The Alexander Pushkin*, which he takes from Montreal to Bremerhaven. He shares a cabin with an Egyptian communist living in Moscow. The

Egyptian greets him with these words: “You have no choice about being Christ.”

“What makes you think that I am Christ?”

“You look a little bit like him. You know, we’ll have to write a book about this some day.”

“The real Christ is in prison.”

Robin now knows for sure what he has always suspected, and that is that Tillich was secretly on the side of the Communists the whole time that he was teaching in American universities. American Christians, who were so delighted to see such a brilliant man writing holy verbiage, never thought that when Tillich talked about socialism, he actually might have a basic loyalty to the international Marxist movement. Robin also feels sorry for his parents, who would not have been pleased to know that when they were paying for his Harvard education, he became involved in a communist conspiracy. He also thinks it bizarre that a Muslim Marxist could dare to make any comments about Christology.

Marxist ethics says that any activity whatsoever is morally justifiable if it advances the cause of the socialist revolution. For Tillich this meant that he could exploit the confusion of a young American schizophrenic and take advantage of his hallucinations to immortalize himself, whilst betraying the country that had allowed him to live in glory and luxury for thirty-two years. One is reminded of these verses from the Gospel:

"Watch therefore; for ye know not what hour your Lord doth come. But know this, that if the goodman of the house had known in which watch the thief would come, he would have watched, and would not have suffered his house to be broken up. Therefore be ye also ready; for in such an hour as ye think not the Son of man cometh." (Matthew 24: 42-44)

On September 27 1975, two thugs, whom Mark had walloped the week before in the prison showers after they tried to rape him, kill him in the gymnasium. They use a 150 pound weight bar to asphyxiate him. In both *Zabriskie Point* and in the Norfolk prison, Mark is killed under the sign of the cross. In the film, he is in a small airplane whose wings are in the shape of a cross. In prison, the bar on his throat while he lies on the bench also makes the form of a cross.

This is the worst day in human history since the crucifixion of Jesus. The Word was made flesh for a second time, and humanity has crucified Christ once again. "Darkness drops again," Yeats says, as his rough beast dies at the age of twenty-seven. The stars fall out of the sky (Matthew 24:29) and the moon and the sun refuse to shed their light. This is the final catastrophe of world history that Tillich prophesied[14]. Of all the horrors that befall Robin in America, this is the most grievous of all.

---

[14] Paul Tillich. *Theology of Peace.* Louisville, Kentucky: Westminster/John Knox Press, 1990, p. 132.

Mark continues to visit Robin in his dreams. His message is always the same: “As you can see, I am still alive. The stories about me dying were all a lie. I have just been in hiding. Now I have come back to you.”

Epilogue: An interview between the author and Robin

"He hath showed thee, O man, what is good; and what doth the Lord require of thee, but to do justly, to love mercy, and to walk humbly with thy God?"
Micah 6:8

Author: First of all, I would like to ask you why you have hired me to be a ghostwriter and write your story for you. Certainly you are able to write yourself. Where was the problem?

Robin: Well, I guess there were two main reasons. First of all, this whole story is so painful for me that I cannot talk about it without getting all upset. How often have you seen me break down weeping when I related incidents from my life in America? I get all flustered when I try to talk about it. Imagine how hard it would be to write about it.

The other reason is that I have been losing my English. For fifty years now I have been living in other languages. For the past forty years, I have spoken mostly French and Spanish. So I am losing my English. Linguists call this linguistic attrition. I am more fluent in French and Spanish than I am in

English, and I have to search for my words in English.

Author: I can understand that you speak French, since you have lived in Rimouski in Quebec for the past forty years, but how come you also speak Spanish a lot?

Robin: I am married to a Cuban man named Juan Lucas. When I came to Rimouski in 1977, I was hired to teach English literature at the University here. The following year Juan Lucas became a Professor of Spanish literature. We soon discovered that we were both gay, and we have been living in a monogamous relationship since 1978. We always speak Spanish together, not only because my Spanish is better than his English, but also because of our three adopted children. In 1981, Juan Lucas, who is a devout Catholic, was contacted by a Catholic charity who informed him of a family of three children in El Salvador whose parents had just been killed in an automobile accident. They suggested that we adopt the kids and we agreed. There were three: Pedro, seven years old, Pablo, who was five and little Isabel, who was just two. When they arrived here, I thought that it would be wonderful for them to learn English. I would only speak to them in English and Juan Lucas would speak to them in Spanish and they would speak French with the kids in the neighbourhood and at school. Then I changed my mind. I thought that it would be easier for them to adjust to their new life in Canada if they only heard Spanish at home and French outside the house.

They had already suffered horrible traumas, losing their parents and then coming to a strange country with a frigid climate, so I thought it would lessen the strangeness of it all for them if they only heard Spanish at home. Of course, they learnt English at school as all children in Quebec do. Pedro and Pablo now live in Montreal and Isabel is a doctor in Quebec City. We have five grandchildren and that is wonderful. Juan Lucas and I were married in the Unitarian Church of Montreal in 1982, and we had a legal wedding in Quebec when gay marriage became possible here in 2004. Let me tell you that the secret of my happiness on this earth is Juan Lucas and our fidelity to each other.

Author: Do you know what happened to Matthew?

Robin: The last time that I saw Matthew was on Commencement Day at Harvard in 1968, this means graduation day. I was walking in front of Lowell House on Mount Auburn Street and I saw Matthew sitting alone on a bench. It was the first time that I had seen him since we were together at McLean Hospital in 1965. I went up to him and spoke to him for the first time since we were roommates together at Exeter in 1962. I just told him, "I am so happy to see you here today."

He stood up and shook my hand and said, "So am I." And that was that. It was really a miracle that he and I managed to graduate in 1968 at the same time as the other boys who had started Harvard with us in 1964, considering how much time he and I had

had to spend in mental hospitals, trying to come to terms with ourselves, and after having had our lives broken by the homophobic psychiatrists at Exeter. Of course I had started Harvard as a sophomore and then I did three summer school sessions, so that explains how I managed to graduate in 1968, but I really have no idea how Matthew managed.

Matthew then went to law school. He committed suicide in 1974 at the age of 28, with a pistol in his mouth. Now here we have the story of two young men who were driven to insanity and suicide by psychiatrists, and no one bats an eye, no one says he's sorry, as though it just did not happen. The psychiatrists walk off with the thousands of dollars they had made in destroying two young lives. No one takes any responsibility. Psychiatrists have no accountability to anyone. The world has lately witnessed stories of the Roman Catholic clergy sexually abusing boys throughout the world. One scandal has led to another. What was once taboo is no longer. When is something similar going to happen to homosexuals who were the victims of homophobic psychiatrists? Certainly Matthew and I were not the only ones. Those who committed suicide are obviously unable to tell their stories, as well as those who became permanently psychotic. But I have recovered from my psychosis, and I would like to tell their story for them.

I would like to remind the world of how much homosexuals have been persecuted. The Jewish religion has been oppressing us for three thousand years and the Christian religion for two thousand. Where are the lions now that we need them?

Today homosexuality is still illegal in 79 countries and it carries the death penalty in five countries.

Author: Have you kept up with Maria Maddalena Pavvi?

Robin: She and I remained close friends until her death in 1998. I managed to find where Mrs. Frechette, Mark's mother, was living in Boston and went to visit her several times. Once I went to see her with Maria Maddalena. Mrs. Frechette and Maria Maddalena both died of cancer at the Brigham and Women's Hospital in Boston in the same year.

Author: What about David Finkelhor? Have you kept up with him?

Robin: Oh yes, we are still good friends and we see each other every summer. He has become the world's foremost expert on child abuse and family violence. His book *Childhood Victimization* was published by Oxford in 2008. I like to tell David that he saved my life, that I was the first abused child whose life he saved. There were four people whose love rescued me from a life of insanity: David Finkelhor, Paul Tillich, Maria Maddalena Pavvi and Mark Frechette.

Author: Do you know anything about Father Laurence Brett, the pedophile priest who started abusing Mark when he was fourteen years old?

Robin: Brett became so notorious for seducing so many boys that the FBI went after him. He was part of the "pass the trash" phenomenon in the Catholic Church. When one school discovered that he had been abusing boys, they just sent him to another school. When the FBI got on his track, he went down to the Caribbean and lived a life of luxury in Martinique, supported by the Church. He died on Christmas Eve 2010 after falling down the stairs at his apartment. I suppose that he was drunk at the time.

Author: There are two incidents in your account of your life with Mark that might seem to be false. The first is that you say you quoted passages of Tillich's Marxist writings to Mark from books that had not even been published at the time you were reading them to Mark.

Robin: The truth of the matter is that I checked out the original German versions of these books from the Widener Library and translated the passages into English for Mark.

Author: The second story that I tend to doubt is your idea that Mark was killed by his fellow inmates. As you know, an investigation was held and they came to the conclusion that it was an accident and that there was no foul play. What makes you think that it was a homicide?

Robin: I have two reasons. The first is that Mark told me that there were two prisoners at Norfolk who had been harassing him. He told me this when I visited him there in 1974. The second reason is that my last psychiatrist, Dr. John Andrew Hollister Perry Hooker, who was serving time at the Concord Prison at the time of Mark's death, told me that there were rumours going around Massachusetts prisons at the time saying that Mark was killed by fellow inmates. The actual way in which Mark died is really not all that important. It is simply a fact that he went into prison at the age of twenty-five a healthy, beautiful young revolutionary and that he came out two years later a cold, stiff cadaver. It was a most ignominious death, like Christ's.

Author: You told me that Tillich thought of you as being "the great unknown One" for whom he had been waiting all his life. What does that mean?

Robin: I am so glad that you asked me that. I was absolutely delighted when I read the autobiography of Tillich's widow, Hannah. It is called *From Time to Time* and was published in 1973. I was amazed and thrilled to find this passage: "One of Paulus's marital jokes was to insist that I was his 'second best.' He called his first best his 'cosmic reservation.' A first best did not exist on earth, he said, but one must reserve a place for the great unknown One who might come, as the Messiah might come at any moment to the waiting Jews." [15] I was exhilarated when I read this statement because it confirms my basic theory, that Tillich's concept of the *kairos* was exactly the same

[15] Hannah Tillich. *From Time to Time.* New York: Stein and Day, 1973, p. 104.

as that of the Greek New Testament, which means the propitious moment in history for the advent of the Messiah. There can be no *kairos* without the Messiah, just as there can be no Messiah without the *kairos*. Tillich and I were working in tandem, in quest for the true Messiah.

Author: Have you discovered anything salacious or scandalous in Tillich's life?

Robin: In her autobiography, Hannah reveals the most astounding aspects of their private life. Their marriage was made in hell. On their wedding night, for example, Tillich left his bride all alone to go and take part in an orgy with his friends. Hardly a way to get off to a good start in a marriage! He was an inveterate adulterer as well as being a cuckold. His wife was openly bisexual. Several times she asked him for a divorce, but he refused because he thought it would tarnish his image as being a man of God. She writes: "Nevertheless, he did not want a divorce. When all his arguments and entreaties failed, he threw himself on the floor, his limbs flailing. He sent his friends to me, imploring me not to divorce him, saying that it would ruin his career."[16]

But the most fascinating thing that I have discovered about Tillich is that he actually confided in his secretary at Harvard that he knew that he was a schizophrenic. This discovery came as an intense satisfaction for me, since I had suspected that

---

[16] Hannah Tillich. *From Time to Time.* New York: Stein and Day, 1973, p. 190.

Tillich was a schizophrenic ever since I started reading him in 1963 at the age of seventeen. I saw that he described with such perfect accuracy what had happened in my first schizophrenic hallucination, my beatific vision, that he must have had a similar experience himself. And then the rest of his work, his numerous books, are all symptoms of his gigantic messiah complex. Here is the passage from his secretary's book that brought me such delight:

"'You know, Paulus,' I said hesitantly, 'I've often wondered how you have kept from becoming schizophrenic.'

At my words, he bolted upright in his chair. 'But that's just it – I am.'

A shocked note of certainty in his voice jolted me. The word I had used in almost a casual fashion, came alive and hung mid air between us, charging the room with a crackling intensity. We both knew that he himself never used psychiatric terms loosely."[17]

Author: You describe Tillich as being a closet Marxist, an inveterate adulterer and a self-proclaimed schizophrenic. How can you admire such a person?

---

[17] Grace Calí. *Paul Tillich First-Hand. A Memoir of the Harvard Years.* Chicago: Exploration Press, 1995, p. 20.

Robin: And a German patriot. Perhaps I should simply say that I forgive him everything simply because he was a German who opposed the Nazis. Or perhaps I should quote what we say in Canada: 'You should not judge a person until you have walked in her moccasins.' But deep down inside, I know that I admire him mostly because he was a schizophrenic like myself and I know how extremely difficult it is to live with schizophrenia. He was a real model for me. And of course I love Tillich for I know that it was his blessing, the beatific smile he gave me that enabled me to survive the horrors of McLean Hospital. I know that he loved me since he recognized in me the only person on earth who had understood the basic secret of his theology, that it is now, in the twentieth century, that the Second Coming of Christ should happen. He recognized my unique form of intelligence at a moment when the rest of the world considered me to be an incurable lunatic. I knew that his confidence in me was a reflection of his faith in God. He made my own faith in God possible, and without that faith, I would probably have been locked up forever in the funny farms, like Émile Nelligan.

Author: You know that I am an atheist, so it seems to me that your faith in God is nothing but a crutch.

Robin: I have got to the point in my life that I actually feel sorry for people who have never felt the need to pray. It seems to me that their lives are so much more superficial than my own.

Author: Are you suggesting that it is better to be schizophrenic than normal?

Robin: It is certainly more difficult, but it is also more interesting. Don't you ever get tired of being normal? How can you listen to the waves of the ocean without hearing God's voice or see a sunset without seeing his art work? You must be really insensitive.

Author: I try to live in reality. You know that there is no proof for the existence of God, and your Phenomenological Proof of God has to be rejected because it describes a schizophrenic hallucination. God does not exist, that is all there is to it.

Robin: Of course God does not exist. But He is. He did not tell Moses: "I exist." He told him: "I am." There is a difference. As Tillich once said, God is above and beyond existence and non-existence. Actually, there are two types of God in Western civilization. There is the philosopher's God, which is an intellectual construct, and then there is the mystic's God, which is a miraculous force that overwhelms the soul and changes the mystic forever. The two have nothing to do with each other although they are called by the same name.

Author: To have access to your mystic's God, you seem to be telling me that I should first become a schizophrenic, and I really do not think that my wife would like that.

Robin: Instead, you might begin by reading the Bible.

Author: I really don't have the time. Why should I be interested in the myths and hallucinations of ancient Hebrew tribes?

Robin: As far as I am concerned, if you have not read the entire Bible, then your atheism is based on ignorance. First read the good book. If you can read all of it and be inspired by absolutely nothing in it, then something is wrong with your soul. You cannot reject God until you have read His book.

Author: Yet I know many experts on classical Greek civilization who have read all of ancient Greek literature and yet do not believe in Zeus.

Robin: As you know, religion is part of the human constitution. In all epochs and cultures people have religions, with their different myths, moral codes, and rituals. By rejecting God and all religions, you atheists also reject humanity and say that you do not want to be part of the human race. You consider yourselves superior to normal people and that is really a form of hubris.

Author: But you really don't sincerely believe that Mark Frechette was the Second Coming of Christ. Come on.

Robin: Of course not. I have no religious beliefs. We Unitarians do not believe in the possibility of a Messiah, in the past, in the present or in the future. The first commandment that Jesus taught us is that we should love God, not that we should believe in Him. If you begin by loving Him, He will change the way you see the world and you will begin to understand that life is not limited to the intellect. *"Le coeur a ses raisons que la raison ne connaît point,"* as Pascal said. The Christian religion is a religion of love. I love God and I know that He loves me. I love Jesus as though he were my personal Saviour. I love Paul Tillich as though he were a true prophet of the living God. And I love Mark Frechette as though he were the Word made flesh for a second time. Love is eternal. I could not stop loving Tillich or Mark just because of the bad things that they did in their lives. My religion is not based on dogmas or doctrines, but on my own existential experience. "For whom the Lord loveth he chasteneth" (Hebrews 12:6).

Author: Why do you want to publicize your own madness?

Robin: I believe that faith in God is a gift from God and that God wants me to share it with others. When I had my vision at age 17, I told myself that I would believe that this was the true God, the God of Abraham, Isaac and Jacob, until my dying day, no matter what other people had to say about it. My religion is not based on intellectual speculation. It is based on existential experience. First reading the entire Bible at ages thirteen and fourteen, then the beatific vision at age seventeen, then receiving Tillich's blessing at age eighteen, then telling Mark Frechette that he was the suffering Christ, and finally Mark's crucifixion. How do you expect me to live with such horrible memories if I do not think that it was God who enabled me to survive all that? For I am a survivor; I have spent the past fifty years without consulting any psychiatrist or taking any psychiatric medicine. That is a real miracle. I would like my own story to be a source of hope for other people who suffer from schizophrenia or any other type of mental illness. I would like them to know that a diagnosis of psychosis does not automatically mean the end of one's life, the end of one's possibility of achieving happiness in this world. I would also like people to know that religious faith is the best psychiatric medicine possible. This means just accepting that God loves us. That's all. Tell yourself over and over again that God loves you and you will be alright.

Author: Well, of course, I think that I am all right as I am. And honestly, your theological hallucinations seem to me to be no more than a "tale told by an idiot, full of sound and fury, signifying nothing." Sorry.

Robin: "The fool hath said in his heart, there is no God." Psalm 14:1.

Author: There you go again being sanctimonious. Can't we keep this discussion a coherent exchange between rational creatures? You say that you and Tillich had a similar kind of schizophrenia. You also say that he had a messiah complex. That means that you too have a messiah complex. What would you do if you were the Messiah?

Robin: Because of Tillich's messiah complex, he thought that the world would return to paradise once German religious socialism had replaced American capitalist imperialism. Although I will always keep socialist ideals in my heart and will always be grateful that I have spent the past fifty years in countries that have socialized medicine, whenever I hear the word "socialism" I have to think of what I lived through in communist Poland and East Germany; the misery, the corruption, the inefficiency, the suppression of fundamental human rights. For Tillich, socialism was a philosophical abstraction, whereas for me it was part of my existential experience.

For my part, my great messianic longing is for peace and a reduction of violence. If I were the Messiah, I would create universal lasting peace simply by requiring nations to respect international law. Governments expect their citizens to follow the law. Now has come the time for citizens to demand that their governments follow the law, international law. This would happen in three steps. First, the United Nations would oblige the nations of the world to respect the most fundamental aspects of existing international law, like refraining from attacking or occupying foreign countries. Secondly, the world would accept the resolutions of the United Nations General Assembly as having the force of international law. Thirdly, the five permanent members of the Security Council would give up their right to a veto. If mankind is clever enough to put a man on the moon, we ought to be clever enough to put an end to warfare.

As for violence in my own unhappy fatherland, I would repeal the Second Amendment, outlaw all firearms other than hunting rifles and require these rifles to be locked up in local police stations during the non-hunting season.

Author: Wow. If I as an atheist am ever asked to vote for the Messiah, you can count on my vote. I would like to let you have the final word in this interview. Are you trying to create a new religion?

Robin: There can be no doubt whatsoever that Tillich wanted to create a new epoch of the Christian religion, and I suppose that I have spent my life trying to do his bidding. You know, once God enters your life, it is impossible to get rid of Him. I am convinced that Tillich would have found Mark Frechette to be a better candidate for being the Parousia, the Second Coming, than I am. Tillich was a closet Marxist, whereas Mark was a real revolutionary. The true Christ is always someone else. You cannot go around saying, "I am the Messiah" because the first rule of a religious person is the vow of humility. All that you can say is that someone else is the Christ.

Author: I think that you should have the last word. What would it be?

Robin: Nations rise and nations fall, but the word of our God shall endure forever.

Author: Thank you for this interview.

Appendices

Robin's letter to Paul Tillich

Harvard, March 27, 1965

The Phenomenological Proof of God

Table of Contents

Chapter 1: Schelling's Dilemma Answered

"Since Kant, there has been so much talk of immanent cognition, immanent knowing and thinking in the favourable sense, and, on the other hand, of the transcendent in the unfavourable sense, that the latter cannot be mentioned without a sort of apprehension or fear. But this fear applies properly only to the standpoint of former metaphysics which we have annulled."
Friedrich Wilhelm Joseph von Schelling

"Philosophy awakens, makes one attentive, shows ways, leads the way for a while, makes ready, makes one ripe for the experience of the uttermost."
Karl Jaspers

Unfortunate as it is, ever since the time of Augustine, Western man has felt a diabolical desire to "prove God," implying what everyone knows to be the impossible: that man, through his "reasoning spectre" could grasp what is, properly, only the concern of the total psyche, or soul. But yet, with this knowledge, we still refuse to have any hope of

His reality. Why this paradox? It is probably due to the tremendous audience given to a nauseating French novel about a philosopher who refused to let his atheistic sentiments change with the growth of his total psyche, or soul. But, perhaps this paradox is all for the best. We know that we cannot "prove" God with our reasoning spectre, yet we also feel a mysterious urge coming from some unknown part of our psyche that says: there is more to life than despair, than anxiety, than bitterness and frustration. It is because man has this intuition that the "proof" that is about to follow should bring him, so to speak, "good news."

Proof of God that does not involve man's reasoning spectre except to the extent that it makes reasonable the otherwise unreasonable? Alas, it seems so absurd. But, then again, my veins tell me that the world wants to hear the magic words: "We have thus proved the reality of God." As though, if I could say this with a certain amount of "intellectual onanism", that their lives would somehow be improved! So, let us begin. Let us "start afresh" with our pagan Greek philosophy so that the Hebraic Spirit will conquer the lands now put to slumber by worshippers of the Dionysian spirit. Is this the end of all Western philosophy? Is this, perhaps, then, the beginning of a new epoch for the European mind? We shall see.

It is a good thing that all ontological, teleological, eschatological, first-mover, Thomistic, Anselmian and Cartesian proofs for the existence of God have fallen into abysmal philosophical disrepute. For any God that can be proved objectively is obviously the creation of the logician's mind, and hardly the Creator of the logician. The God that St. Thomas, with such good intentions, tried to prove, we shall call Urizen, William Blake's name for the God of orthodox theism. The God that I shall "prove" must, by the very nature of the "proof," be the true God. The question naturally arises in the reader's mind as to just how I shall go about proving that which no reasoning spectre can comprehend. The method, itself, is so simple, so obvious to me that I find it surprising that it has not been attempted before. It is the phenomenological epoché of Edmund Husserl. He has told us, "There will be no psychical existence whose 'style' we shall not know." I am here accepting this offer von Herrn Husserl. I shall reveal my own "psychical style," for whatever good it may do the reader. But before I begin that, I would like to examine the psychical style of ordinary man, to see what it has to offer the Western mind. I am speaking of the mind of the non-mystic.

Husserl has explained to us that we can know for certain only that which we experience subjectively. In other words, we are being naïve to accept anything other than that with which our mind comes into immediate contact. By a radical Cartesian process of doubt, Husserl has convinced the West that we should limit our concept of "knowledge" to that which can be grasped as being apodictically true in the immediate situation. As psychic phenomena pass through our minds, we should always realize that all the knowledge that is important, all that we should consider in our phenomenological and transcendental reductions, are the psychic representations that are, so to speak, "there."

Blake once said that Jesus represented the full spiritual maturation of the Jewish nation. Likewise, we can conceive of Edmund Husserl as representing the fullest possible maturation of the Greek rational search for "knowledge." (Let us give thanksgiving that that search has now been ended and will never again be resumed on the face of the Hebraic God's earth. Oh, don't think I don't love Aeschylus and Euripedes and Sophocles and Socrates. I do. But there is something about the Greek Dionysian spirit that does not seem as much a Creator or as eternal as does the Hebraic (the God of Abraham, Jesus, Pascal, Whitman and Tillich). (It also seems that, as of today, there will be no more Greek-minded Urizen-worshipping theologians.)

So, let us digress no further, and simply state what Husserl has made obvious for us: it is impossible for the non-mystic to give us any knowledge of 'Being' as a whole. Now, the question comes: is it ever possible, with our phenomenological epoché, to come to "grips" with "reality as a whole"?

I think that there is. I shall attempt to show that, through a phenomenological reduction of a mystical ecstatic vision, we can go directly from and through subjective knowledge to knowledge of the supra-objective. Through knowledge of the supra-objective! A strange theory of knowledge in a Greek civilization! Let us, then, imagine the mystic who is undergoing his Divine Vision. He naturally thinks that he is "seeing things," so he rubs his eyes, so to speak (to take account of that which is "passing before" him). No matter how much he tries to doubt, to close his eyes, to tell himself, "No, this thing cannot be happening to me, a wretched sinner!" he is incapable of doubting the following: (which can be regarded as the *cogitati* of the *Evidenz* of the psychic situation):

1) This is the eternal nature of reality.
2) Being is "inside and outside" divine.
3) When these psychic representatives pass, the ones that shall follow will be, in some sense, wrong, illusory.

What, then, is our conclusion? Our conclusion is that, through the phenomenological approach to knowledge, we have found that the only time a person can "come to grips with" Being is when he is in a mystical ecstasy. Then alone is truth revealed. This, then, our final conclusion (which will be explained further in Part C of Chapter 3): God is the only reality; any non-theistic concept of Being, then, is illusory.

If this chapter has raised the Spirit of the West, then it is only because the Greek West has never understood the nature of its Hebraic God. If Jesus were alive today, he would be glad to know that we have at last buried his never-heard-of arch rivals: Plato and Aristotle.

Chapter 2: Purgation through Existential Anxiety and Despair

"Ich denke oft, vielleicht ist Gottes Hand wieder unterwegs."
Rainer Maria Rilke"

I began my mystical life in hell.

Being a Sartre-admiring atheist for two years at least, I kept telling myself, "You are free to do whatever you want!" But then I would be interrupted by a voice that would haunt me saying, "What the hell good does it do to be free to do things, if I am not even capable of just being alive? Let the living do absurd things for the living. But the dead know that only the dead are worth looking after! The dead for the dead! The living for the living! And I, I the dead, I in the one, the only one, the sole grave in this cemetery called death. It has been said that the dead should bury their dead. The dead has just buried himself.

I alone am guilty. It is I alone who has put myself into eternal hell. This is my self-inflicted punishment for my immature self-destructiveness, this is all that I will ever be able to be, this is all that I will ever deserve to be: a self-destroying wanderer in hell.

"Can another layer of death suddenly open up? To receive me, its guest-to-be, into its deeper abyss!

"Sartre is right. I have chosen this. I have chosen to condemn myself to eternal hell. I am incapable, or unwilling, to choose more for myself than self-destruction. I deserve this never ending death. I have chosen my crime, my crime which is its own punishment.

"Yes. But no. No! No, I did not choose all of this. I certainly did not choose this passion of mine. This passion to destroy myself! This is no creation of mine! I could never deliberately do this to myself. That I can never say. No! Fated from birth for this! Perhaps it was I that gave into this passion – there is my guilt! But I, I, I, forever to be a self-condemned wanderer in hell.

Then there were brief moments of surrendering in exhaustion to the despair. It was like Shelley's famous lines:

Yet now despair itself is mild,

Even as the winds and waters are;

I could lie down like a tired child,

And weep away the life of care

Which I have borne and yet must bear,

Till death like sleep might steal on me,

And I must feel in the warm air

My cheek grow cold, and hear the sea

Breathe o'er my dying brain its last monotony.

But anxiety over the thought that I had surrendered to despair soon revived the more violent aspects of despair.

Right before plunging headlong into absolute death, for this is all that the spirit's eyes can see ahead during absolute despair – absolute death – right before this. Ah, well, for the continuation of this exciting narrative, the reader is asked to wait until we come to Chapter 3.

This stage of the mystic's life I call "Purgation of all Ultimate Ends through Existential Anxiety and Despair." By this is meant simply that the participant realises that there is nothing worth living for. He can find no purpose for his life. He does not object to occupying alone the only grave in the cemetery called death. He does not object! But, then again, why should he? There is no God left in our universe, and if there were one he would be too distant to be of any help. Everybody around him who is alive is deceiving himself, he is telling himself that there is something worth living for. They are guilty of the worst kind of lifelong lies: the lie of denying, through cowardice and lack of honesty, the absolute absurdity of all existence. They are unheroic scum!

This stage of the mystic's life can be seen as an almost necessary prerequisite for further advancement. Blaise Pascal suffered from it so much: he knew he should mortify himself for this was the will of God, but his physical self-laceration would not have taken on the qualities of existential despair had it not been for the haunting, mocking comments of his atheist friends. Without this existential despair, Pascal would never have had a Divine Vision.

Much of the same anxiety that I experience can be seen in the life of the young St. Francis, although his was undoubtedly less than mine since, we can be sure, he never doubted the reality of God. His anxiety was simply over what his relationship with Him should be. Evelyn Underhill, the unchallenged expert on Western mysticism, describes St. Francis's earlier life thus: "His mind, in modern language, had not unified itself. He was a high-spirited boy, full of vitality: a natural artist, with all the fastidiousness which the artistic temperament involves. War and pleasure both attracted him, and upon them, says his legend, he 'miserly squandered and wasted his time.' Nevertheless, he was vaguely dissatisfied. In the midst of festivities he would have sudden fits of abstraction: abortive attempts of the growing transcendental consciousness, still imprisoned below the threshold but aware of and in touch with the Real, to force itself to the surface and seize the true." (p. 180).

Miss Underhill also mentions Catherine of Genoa as having sunk into "a state of dull wretchedness; a hatred of herself and of life," before her first encounter with the Divine.

The point of this chapter is to state that, before any mystical encounter with God can be realized, there must be a process of dying-unto-oneself. God will not shed his love on those who have other ultimate ends in life than Himself. He will not let a person worship mammon and at the same time taste, within this life, an enduring participation within His Spirit. And without participation in His Spirit in this life, it is impossible to understand what has been called Life Eternal.

Chapter 3: The Divine Vision

Part A: The Experience Itself

"And the Lord answered me, and said, Write the vision, and make it plain upon tables, that he may run that readeth it."
Habakkuk 2:2

Back to our narrative. Suddenly I felt something in me, so strange, I had not felt anything like it within my two years of being a Sartre-admiring atheist. I felt, from within, a desire to pray. Now, this may seem like a natural thing to do when one is in hell. But for a person who is proud of being among the enlightened group of his generation, a group made up solely of atheists, such a desire is a terrible disgrace. It is a sign of one's weakness, one's cowardice, one's inability to undergo the hell that we have been told we chose to create. Nothing is more unheroic for the atheist than the recognition that he has resorted to the desire to pray. Nothing!

So, I said it: (Yes, I chose to say it): "God." (When one is in hell, all words are internal more than external.) Once this word had been said, from within, there was a feeling of my soul being pulled and pulled and pulled. There is no situation analogous to it in Western literature, I believe. The soul is pulled and pulled and pulled, from one layer of hell up into the next, and higher, and higher, so suddenly, so unexpectedly, without the participant's knowing or controlling what is happening, pulled, pulled, until, at last: the ecstatic vision of the Divine.

During this absolute ecstatic state, and after the first shocking seconds in it, the participant tries to recover his "senses." "How can I see this unbearable brightness before me – a brightness of infinite depth – when there is no sunlight even?" He turns his corporeal eyes from the brightness just to re-assure himself that he still has his physical existence. But, he sees, his senses are not "playing tricks" on him. Wherever he turns his eyes, he sees that all of being is alive with Divinity. Everything appears, in itself, infinite and eternal. Everything is unified, and the participant is unified with everything. Now he returns his eyes to that brightness that he had felt he could never endure seeing again. The brightness continues until the ecstasy ends, which has to be within minutes, for the soul's psychic energy is hardly inexhaustible.

But what has he seen within that brightness? Need I be more explicit: "What is the nature of God?" The question that has puzzled man since the beginning of time! And, here he is, closer to knowing the answer, closer than anyone in history!

He has been "let in" on all the secrets of the cosmos. That which has always been and always shall be is now revealed.

In the first place, the "inner essence" of God is not revealed. It is as though there were a veil of a million angels preventing the participant from seeing that which He is. Imagine staring at the sun. Your corporeal eye will not let you. Imagine staring straight into the totality of God. Your spiritual eye will not let you. Blake once said that in his Divine Vision he saw "as it were, only the hem of their garments." Of course there are no "they," no garments, and no hems; but Blake explains it quite well.

Although this is hardly what Kierkegaard has in mind when he quoted, for us, Lessing's words, it is appropriate to restate them now. (I like them so much I'd state them any time, anyway.)

"Wenn Gott in seiner Rechten alle Wahrheit, und in seiner Linken den einzigen immer regenden Trieb nach Wahrheit, obschon mit dem Zusatz mich immer und ewig zu irren, verschlossen hielte, und spräche zu mir: wähle! Ich fiele ihm mit Demut in seine Linke und sagte, Vater, gieb! Die reine Wahrheit ist ja doch nur für Dich allein!"

Certain aspects of God's nature, however, can be stated quite briefly. For example, the life of this planet, in His "eyes" is but a fraction of a second. If this can be understood, then the reader has approached comprehension of the nature of His Eternity. Also, as Dr. Tillich has so well observed, it is He alone that gives the power of being to all that has being. This is seen so strongly, but it is so hard to communicate. Perhaps this would be a good analogy: a person who knows nothing about the physicist's theories of electricity suddenly *sees* all the electricity coming from the city's generator to light up all the city's street lights. Without God, there would be no Being. God is seen as being infinite. Infinite in the sense that He encompasses the infinity of Being; He permeates it, so to speak. But there is also that additional part of Him that transcends Being. (How many infinite parts make up the infinite, Leibnitz?) Thus, we can say that God consists of: The Power of God, which permeates all physical being to give it its being, and which also animates all life; the transcendent Spirit of God, which, as later becomes evident to the mystic, is participated in by two individual humans whenever they make genuine psychological contact, thus, as Dr. Tillich has observed, assisting in the psychosexual development and fulfillment of each human being; and, finally, that "part" of God which, so to speak, transcends His transcendent Spirit, that of Him which is never known, never touched, always distant, always incomprehensible. Although Dr. Tillich's theology does not recognize this aspect of the Divine, his sermons seem to show that his mind actually intuits it. It is this which is neither spirit nor power that makes a person justified in feeling that God is always "watching" him.

It is easy for the non-mystic to think that God consists of three separate layers of matter-like substance. This is false for the simple reason that God can never be seen with just the corporeal eye. The three "parts" of Him are all, spatially speaking, interfused. St. John of the Cross has, with much perception, said that God is like "an infinite circle whose centre is everywhere and whose circumference is nowhere." In other words, there is no one place on the earth that you can go to without God being there before and while you are going there.

The reader is begged not to think that when God makes himself manifest, He jumps down from some place in the sky. God, let it be said, merely opens the spiritual eye of the participant to one infinite part of his greater infinity. And in that one infinite part, all the details of his eternal nature that man can grasp, all of these are given.

There were two feelings during this experience that need to be stated. First: "Where, my God, is thy respect for thine own law? Surely Thou dost know that I am the lowest of the lowest, the guiltiest of the guilty, and yet it is Thou that hast revealed these wonders to me." Secondly: it was quite surprising to see that God is not a passive onlooker who steps down from the stars occasionally to occupy a seat behind a secret altar in a secret temple; that, indeed, he permeates all and directs all, all…. All except the human mind and human action.

Also, I would like to state for our philosophers interested in the peculiar technique of our first chapter, that it was when the mystic removed his eyes from the brightness in front of him to be able to take account of the situation, it is then that he, so to speak, performs his phenomenological reduction of the situation.

There were three other sensations that will become meaningful as we progress in this discussion. ("Sensations" is a bad word for what is revealed in a visionary ecstasy, but it will have to suffice, for I refuse to use traditional terms like "revelations.") I remember feeling how glad I had been that I had passed through that long and unbearable hell. Without it, I knew, I would never have *seen.* There is a terrible price one must pay to be able to *see* what is seen in the vision of the Divine, but, yet, one is willing to pay the price. Why? Suso, the medieval German mystic, expressed this thus: "If that which I see and feel be not the Kingdom of Heaven, I know not what it can be: for it is very sure that the endurance of all possible pains were but a poor price to pay for the eternal possession of so great a joy."

The second important "sensation" that is worth mentioning was that of being given a very special and incomprehensible favour from God. As though it was partially out of kindness and partially to test me to see what I would "make of" the experience. There is always the feeling "why me, damn it all?" But asking "Why me" hardly relieves one of the burden, it merely replaces it with another burden: the despair of guilt, of knowing that there is a virtue and a sin in this one instance that no legalistic system of seven sins and seven virtues can encompass, or can approve or condone or condemn.

Before we continue this small book, I would like to indulge in a little bit of eloquence to let the reader know that I'm not dropping down from the sky suddenly, to let him know that I do know something about the atheistic despair of our times, that, in fact, my life has reflected more of that despair than any "well-adjusted" atheist is ever asked to endure.

To all Jews and Christians and anyone else that would love His God, I should like to say this: the God of our fathers, of Whom we sing so reluctantly in church on Sunday but to whom we pray so hard when we are on our death beds, He has not forgotten us, we who (to our knowledge) are the only creatures of His Creation who have ever had any faith in Him. He still sees us and our needs. He has seen our present despair and fear. He has not forsaken us. As in ancient days, even today, He is willing to lead us out of the land of bondage. As He once led us out of Egypt, now He is ready to help us lead ourselves out of the bondage of fear and meaninglessness and despair and guilt and world-suicide. My knowledge that He has not forgotten us, this alone gives me the right (and the obligation) to write this.

I would now like to discuss, by way of contrast, and for the purpose of drawing a moral, the divine Vision of one of the best friends that French literature has given me: Blaise Pascal.

Aldous Huxley, who naively and tragically assumed that every mystical phenomenon in the world was somehow related to mescaline mysticism, once showed his lack of understanding of mysticism when he wondered why Pascal's writing had contained so much discussion of misery and pain. I shall attempt to answer Huxley's question.

Pascal was naturally religious, as some of us are, perhaps just because of psychological factors. He felt that the need for developing a perfect relationship with God was more urgent than any other need. So he mortified himself, saying that it was for God that he was doing this. He not only wanted to show God how obedient he was to Him, but he also wanted to impress his atheist friends with his fidelity. Now, Pascal's image of God was undoubtedly that of the theistic God, Whom Blake has named Urizen. This was hardly Pascal's fault; it had been the image that society had perpetuated of God since the Christians exchanged their ultimate aim of life, which had been the Ever-Present God, to appeasing Urizen by worshipping church officials. So, let us not blame my friend Pascal for worshipping Urizen. Pascal realized, of his own free will, that his relationship with his God was not satisfactory. He realised this in suffering and anguish, which he himself felt were the proper ways for him to worship his God. Because he realised that his relationship with God was unsatisfactory, he forced himself to suffer; God, whose justice is without question and comprehension, rewarded

Pascal with a Vision of His Wonders. The Vision was rewarded because God knew that Pascal had a pure heart and was desirous of serving the real God. Thus, God did show that He was not distant, up in the stars, as the Urizen-worshippers say, but that he was ever-present, always close to Pascal. Let us listen to the words of Pascal's famous *Mémorial:*

Feu – comme celui de Moïse,

Dieu d'Abraham, Dieu d'Isaac, Dieu de Jacob, mais non des philosophes et des savants.

Pascal is here telling us that God is not like the God preached by most ministers; not like the God dissected by most theologians.

Does Pascal, the most brilliant religious mind of France, doubt this? No!

Certitude. Certitude.

Is he in hell or in heaven when he is seeing this God?

Sentiment, Joie. Paix.

To make it certain that God is not what Urizen-worshippers suppose Pascal adds:

Père juste, le monde ne t'a point connu, mais je t'ai connu.

We see: *Le père est juste, même pour Pascal, pécheur misérable.*

Pascal, who had one of the worst guilt complexes ever, has just been granted a vision of the Divine! What does this mean for the orthodox concept of God as judge-jury-executioner all rolled into one? It means this: no matter who you are, no matter what you have done, what race you are, what language you speak, what national and state laws you have broken, God is willing to accept you into His Spirit and into His Kingdom, a Kingdom which, once it has been entered, gives to the participant knowledge of the true nature of that which has been called Life Eternal. All that you must do is to humble yourself, spiritually, before the Ever-Present God. If you can find that one small ounce of humility, all is not lost for you or for your civilization and your world.

Now we come to the sad ending of his *Mémorial. Je m'en suis séparé; je l'ai fui, renoncé, crucifié.* From then on, Pascal knew only the same "old" guilt. He thinks that he has killed God because the Vision has vanished. Well, poor Pascal did not realise that a vision can last only a short while, (only as long as the ecstasy lasts) and that the ecstasy cannot last forever because it depends on one's own supply of psychic energy, which is certainly not inexhaustible. So Pascal becomes guilty again and, in his mind, he once again conceives of God as looking like Urizen. He suffers his life out until he dies, and on his death bed he feels guilty about not having helped the poor enough. Until Pascal died, we must remember, he carried within his doublet his little *Mémorial* which he had written during and after his ecstasy. We must imagine Pascal telling himself, from the time of his vision to the time of his death: "No matter how much I have suffered during my lifetime, it has all been made up for by this (pointing to his *Mémorial*)." But it wasn't "made up for": Pascal, on his death bed, was afraid. And, for those who have entered the Kingdom of God *in this lifetime* (which is the prerequisite for being able to understand the nature of that which is called Life Eternal), there is no fear at death. This is the moral of this tragic story of a good friend of mine whom we have just discussed: never, never, never be satisfied with your relationship with the Ever-Present God. If you become satisfied, if you try to appease the real God by inventing father-image gods or by worshipping man or merely lighting candles or by simply participating in church activities, you will never discover, in this lifetime, the Kingdom of our Father, a Kingdom which, we were told 2000 years ago, we must seek out and find.

Chapter 3, Part B: The Commands

It is embarrassing for me to write of the commands that were revealed to me during my ecstatic vision. Embarrassing because I hope that it will be one of my victories, when I die, to be able to look back over my lifetime and see that the world has become convinced that there is no such thing as an eternal moral law. We know that Moses, in his ecstatic vision, decided to make the Ten Commandments the law of Israel. It is because of Moses and the ancient Hebrews that, in our Judaeo-Christian religious traditions, we still find sects preaching "eternal moral laws." I shall attempt to convince who would listen that Moses's giving of the Ten Commandments has been greatly misunderstood. During an ecstatic vision, God does not tell the participant anything. But in that ecstasy, in that condition of being face to face with the sole Truth, the supreme Right, one is able to understand so much more about the nature of the world and about what one must do. Moses, during his Vision, which came at a personal and national *kairos*, knew that his people needed a law. They were, as we all know, an unruly bunch, worshipping calves and what not.

God did not give Moses the Ten Commandments one after another. He did not conjure up golden plates and scratch miraculous Hebrew characters onto them. How, then, did we get the Ten Commandments?

It must be remembered that 1) Moses had grown up in Egypt in the Egyptian court; 2) that he had been taught the law of that pagan country; and 3) that the Egyptian Book of the Dead contains a law that included ten commandments that are exactly the same as our ten. Here is our evidence. What are we to make of it? Israel, in Moses's day, needed a legalistic system, so Moses, in the perfect wisdom which is a part of any Divine Vision, decided to give to Israel the law of Egypt.

That was what God's Nation needed in Moses's day. Let us ask ourselves, "What does God's nation need today?" We look around us and we see millions of lives being destroyed by guilt. (Does God want to destroy that which He alone is also creating?) Why do we feel guilt? We feel guilt because the leaders of our society have, through the churches, convinced us that the laws that they legislate in state-houses are also the law of God. (They do not worship our Lord, however; most of them have made their political careers their gods.) Our leaders have made us believe in a father-image type god who, they say, will punish us in an afterlife if we do not obey the laws that they legislate. We have listened to this too long! This kind of self-righteous nonsense is destroying the spirit of the only civilization which has been constantly mindful (in varying degrees) of the world's Creator. We will have no more of it!

Now, perhaps, we should look at Jesus and the law that he preached. He preached one law: love and mutual acceptance and forgiveness. This is the law that Jesus has told us is the only divine law. He has told us that if we followed it, we would obtain what we must obtain: the Kingdom of God on Earth as it is in Heaven. (Although Heaven is not up in the stars, it is the home of God; we know this because it is impossible for anyone to encounter God, in any way, unless that person is, himself, in heaven.) We have been told over and over again by great religious leaders that Jesus is right. That love and mutual forgiveness are the only divine laws and that we must follow them if we are to obtain our Father's Kingdom upon this Earth! We have been told this not only by Jesus, but also by St. Augustine, St. Francis, William Blake, Martin Buber and Paul Tillich. Now, here is my question: which law have we followed, Moses's or Jesus's? And where has it brought us? To the Kingdom of God or the Kingdom of Mammon? Do we forgive our murderers or do we execute them? Are all our Lord's nations living in peace one with another, or are they building up bombs and hiding them in fear?

With this introduction, I shall go on to mention the commands that I discovered during my own ecstasy. How are commands given? It is sort of combination of having the knowledge screamed into one's brain and also just seeing what has become so obvious. What were the commands? Simply: Have absolute faith in your Lord, Who has just opened our spiritual eye to His Wonders! And: Your love for everyone must also be absolute. (We will remember that Jesus told us that we should *love* our Lord. In this, too, have we failed him: it is still the style to say, "I am a God-*fearing* man.") Let us examine these one at a time. Faith: All that matters is God. All else, for one thing, is so ephemeral. Before Him Who, in the flashing of a second, observes the rising and falling of civilizations? "What kind of audacity does it take, on my part, to think that all my worries and fears and guilt and anxieties are important? All that is important is He!" This is what is meant by faith.

Now, how do we love our neighbour? We realise that we have, ourselves, no individual identity, that we are all a part of the same divine Soul which gives spiritual life to all of us, and more to those that are humble before the Ever-Present God. We know that we cannot kill another, for in killing someone else, we are also killing ourselves. We cannot even hurt another, for his pain will be our pain. The American who, perhaps, lived most strongly within the Spirit of God was Walt Whitman. Let us listen to what he would tell us of the nature of Cosmic Love (*agape)*:

"You laggards there on guard! Look to your arms!

In the conquer'd door they crowd! I am possess'd!

Embody all presences outlaw'd or suffering,

See myself in prison shaped like another man,

And feel the dull unintermitted pain.

For me the keepers of convicts shoulder their carbines and keep watch,

It is I let out in the morning and barr'd at night."

Have we, as Jesus told us we must, loved our neighbour as ourselves? Are we able, like Walt Whitman, to look at a prisoner and say, "His pain is my pain; his loss of life is my loss of life?" Or do we instead prefer to pretend that we have no prisons, or that the lives of our prisoners are not our concern, but only the concern of the state governments? (My anarchist friends want me to advocate the abolition of all prisons. I will not, yet. We are not ready for it, yet. Oh, yes, the prisoners themselves are ready! I work with them and know that they are ready. But is the rest of society? No! Why not? Our worship of him who has been called mammon will not allow us to spend enough money to build decent living conditions for our poor, decent enough to prevent the poor man's hatred of the rich and their natural desire to seek revenge.) This is what is meant by love.

Chapter 3, Part C: The Problem of Interpretation and Illusion

"My soul is a monastery and I am its monk."
Keats

The fact that it has been generally assumed today that only schizophrenics "see God" has made the problem of interpreting my Vision a rather indelicate task.

The act of inner interpretation itself begins when the mystic thinks that he has lost his senses. Moses does the same thing when he realises that the bush itself is not on fire. He looks at it first with his corporeal eye and then with his spiritual eye until he realises that it is a necessity that he believe his spiritual eye and not his corporeal eye. Indeed, Moses began his task of interpretations when he asked "I am" who He was.

I mention Moses often for the simple reason that I, in my vanity, find our situations analogous. The vision for him came at both a personal and national *kairos.* Mine certainly came at a time of personal crisis, and it is my contention, at a time of crisis in the Judaeo-Christian religious tradition. Alas! Let that be my excuse for revealing more of what happens in a mystical vision than anyone else in history! What a traitor to our noble tradition of silence on the subject! Our pet toys with which we could play even until we died! Perhaps, as the Bible suggests, there will be a great deal of frantic running in our civilization because of it. (I shall later write a great deal about the crisis of our civilization, and especially about its fear; let it be said, now, that a great deal of fear has had to be overcome in writing this book.)

Let us consider the question of illusion. It would be easy for me to say, with false timidity and pride: "Here I must take refuge in the stance of the phenomenologist and say that I will let no non-participant in my mind come between me and the *cogitatii* of my consciousness; that I will not compromise my self-dignity by letting a Freudian re-ify my consciousness." But I cannot do this, simply because I am convinced of this: God is the only reality, and all else is illusion. For example, the ordinary mind can see in a pen only something with which to write, but if his "doors of perception were opened," as Blake would say, he would see the pen as participating, itself, within the divine Infinite. There is also this argument: If the layman were not so concerned with mammon, he would be able to discover the Presence of the Eternal Divine Love.

The psychologist might say that my vision was merely the workings of a weak mind that needed a psychological boost to cheer itself up. But I cannot believe this, either, for the simple reason that the vision has made it impossible for me to enjoy all the delectable pleasures in which my contemporaries so love to indulge themselves.

If I were to think that the Vision were a creation of my psyche and not an act of God's will, then I would have to consider my psyche, at that moment, super-human, in order to have created such a self-overwhelming drama. ("Teacher, can a psyche be super-human without being of God?" "Read your abnormal psychology textbook, student, and stop asking stupid questions.").

Alas, now that we have ruled out the possibility of illusion, we can look back in retrospect, and ask ourselves what led up to the experience. I like to think that there were three factors that brought about the Vision: firstly, the appropriate psychological, infernal wanderings; secondly, the willingness on my own part to say, internally, "God"; and thirdly, the will of God. Most Protestant theologians throughout our history have said that all such phenomena are dependent solely on the will of God. I cannot believe this myself. I cannot believe that I was, in any way forced into the Vision. But then again, we should not think that if a man is in absolute despair and that if he humbles himself before any image of God, he will be granted admittance to the Kingdom. The younger Nietzsche and Kierkegaard, both, are examples of this.

The above part of the essay was written before Robin met Tillich. It is useless to reproduce what he wrote after the meeting since it is simply unmitigated delirium.

Robin's letter to Mark Frechette

Bonn, April 12, 1974

Dear Mark,

I have heard through the trans-Atlantic grapevine that you intend to plead insanity. The last thing that I would want to do would be to take the side of the District Attorney, but I must say that you seem to me to be an island of sanity surrounded by an ocean of insanity. You have a logic of your own, which you apply courageously and persistently against all odds. You are a heroic person in a society that allows no heroes. You are a visionary. You have a vision of a world at peace where people are able to love each other because they can respect themselves and see themselves reflected in their fellow human beings. But you live in a society torn apart by hatred and fear and competitiveness. You are a person with a prophetic insight into the requirements of the human soul, not just the individual soul, but the communal soul. But you live in a community that has sacrificed all spiritual values to the materialistic pursuit of dollars, that has reduced all human endeavour to the accumulation of dishwashers and Oldsmobiles and idiot boxes, that has made people think of other people as things, as means for their own materialistic self-advancement. You have seen through the American capitalist system to the horrors underneath the glittering surface, and because you could not give up your visionary ideals of what the good life should be and could be, you were forced to rebel. Robbing your local bank to protest against Watergate was not an insane stunt; it was perhaps the only example of self-sacrificial heroic idealism that I myself have had any personal experience of in twentieth century America. You, like all other visionaries who are crucified by the criminality of the society against which their righteous indignation forces them to rebel, are the suffering Christ. You are also the true American patriot: the soldier of justice ready to risk his life as an example of the heroism needed to counteract the folly of American life.

And, if they do send you away to Bridgewater with a sentence of anything from one day to life, at the discretion of the Commonwealth of Massachusetts to decide when you have succeeded in becoming "sane," what will the psychiatrists be like that attempt to "cure" you? They will have gone to medical school and studied biology and chemistry, with which they will attempt to understand the mysteries of the human mind. They will probably never have had a profound experience of life outside America, and thus will have no idea of what it means to be a healthy member of a healthy society, with all the traditions and homogenous culture and accepted standards of behaviour and manners that make up life in sane, non-American societies. Your psychiatrist will probably have come from a bourgeois American background, will have kissed his first girl after his senior prom in his local high school, will have gone to a second-rate college and second-rate medical school, and today is enjoying a life of golf and bridge clubs and wife-swapping and Sunday school and outdoor barbecues, while being completely oblivious to the social injustice and spiritual bewilderment and indignity and humiliation of the quarter of American citizens who are forced to spend their lives in slums like Roxbury, just as he is oblivious to the thousands of Vietnamese peasants Wall Street is killing for the sake of maintaining its capitalist imperialist grip on the Third World. Is your psychiatrist a sane man?

No, Mark, do not let them tell you that you are insane. You never have been and you never will be. Your acts of bravery seem like insanity to those who haven't the courage to see the truth of "the American way of life" and to act accordingly by rebelling just as you have rebelled. I have always admired you, and perhaps now more than ever.

But I was horrified, when I visited you in September in prison and when I received your hysterical note in January, to see that you apparently consider me one of your innumerable enemies. This, alas, did not seem sane to me. It pained me immensely. Why do you feel this way about me? Is it because I am a successful member of the bourgeoisie? (Can't you see that the German university lecturer costume I put on is only part of an act that gives me the opportunity to put my thoughts about America together, with a better perspective, and the calm necessary to come to terms with all the horrors that I experienced there?) Perhaps I am a coward for having left America. But, please do not forget that I once experienced something very similar to what you are going through now. I was locked up for fifteen months in mental hospitals in America, and I was forced to go there because I too had a vision of a society at peace with itself, made up of members who sought their happiness in their interpersonal relationships, and not in the acquisition of things, and this vision was being frustrated at every turn by what I saw of American life. During those fifteen months of incarceration, I told myself that the first goal I would set for myself in life would be never to come back to a mental hospital again. I am just as insane now as I ever was. I am still convinced that my schizophrenic hallucination of eleven years ago was a beatific vision of divine truth; and I know that this belief must be judged insane by all materialistically "realistic" psychiatrists who attempt to understand the human mind with their scientific formulae and their statistics. I am only pretending to be sane. I would much rather spend my time contemplating divine beauty than participating in the commerce of man's world. But it's more than a game. I'm gathering evidence of what men have made of God's creation. As soon as I'm settled in Montreal in September, I'll probably start making plans for visiting Mexico and Cuba, not just to improve my Spanish, but also to investigate the revolutionary situation there.

I have been dedicated to the principles of pacifism as long as I have known the definition of the word. I am unable to become aggressive with people. I would prefer to let people continue in their folly than to make a fool of myself by trying to correct them. So I am a selfish coward and you are a magnanimous hero. And that is why society considers you insane, as it once did me, and that's how I've managed to get lectureships in two European universities.

The ugly reality, my dear Mark, is that both you and I are condemned forever to live among a race of creatures whose intelligence and sensitivity and sense of justice are vastly inferior to our own. You have your way of dealing with this dilemma, and I have mine. But I would be the last person to suggest that I have been more successful than you.

Perhaps all I want is for you to tell me that you're not completely disgusted with me, that there is some hope that I can do something to redeem our friendship. For you are more important to me than the entire German nation. The experience that I had with you, painful as it was, taught me the identity of the stuff of which I am really made. When I saw you last February you said, in your indelicate way, that you had "fucked me up." This is not the point. The point is that through my experience with you, I was able to learn, for the first time, what my real nature was and where it could lead. One of the reasons that I gave up the gay scene a few years ago was that I finally had the courage and honesty to admit to myself that I was simply looking for a replacement for Mark Frechette, and the search was both futile and an offence to my dignity. I shall always be grateful to you. How long must I be frustrated by not knowing what I can do to show my gratitude? Please write to me.

I wonder if you are allowed to see my letters. Dear Mr. Screw, Are you reading this letter before Mark sees it? If you object to the subversive and perverse contents of the letter and won't allow Mark to see it, would you please write to me and tell me so, so that I won't waste the time of writing other letters like this in the future. It would be much easier to write letters like: Dear Mark, the weather is beautiful, wish you were here.

How do you like the books I am sending you? You must remember that Eldridge Cleaver developed one of the most powerful intellects of the 20th century by the self-education he gave himself in prison. I expect no less from you.

Here's a poem by the Irish poet Yeats, called "The Second Coming," which I recited to myself as the Harvard Police dragged me off to the insane asylum 16 months before Maria Maddalena and I discovered you standing in front of the Harvard Coop. It is about you. You are the rough beast.

Turning and turning in the widening gyre

The falcon cannot hear the falconer;

Things fall apart; the centre cannot hold;

Mere anarchy is loosed upon the world,

The blood-dimmed tide is loosed, and everywhere

The ceremony of innocence is drowned;

The best lack all conviction, while the worst

Are full of passionate intensity.

Surely some revelation is at hand;

Surely the Second Coming is at hand.

The Second Coming! Hardly are those words out

When a vast image out of *Spiritus Mundi*

Troubles my sight: somewhere in sands of the desert

A shape with lion body and the head of a man,

A gaze blank and pitiless as the sun,

Is moving its slow thighs, while all about it

Reel shadows of the indignant desert birds.

The darkness drops again; but now I know

That twenty centuries of stony sleep

Were vexed to nightmare by a rocking cradle,

And what rough beast, its hour come round at last,

Slouches towards Bethlehem to be born?

Love, Robin

Mark's reply to Robin

4/27/74

Dear Robin,

We didn't plead insanity, we pleaded guilty and there was no deal involved. So, the judge followed the DA's recommendation of 6-15 at Walpole. But we probably won't wind up there. I got the book you sent about Chile – haven't had the time to read it yet.

I dug your letter, man, when you say it you really say it.

Take care.

Mark